To the Stadium
Lama Temple
The A's House
Ghost Street
AF730086
To the film's studio

CHINESE WHISKERS

CHINESE WHISKERS

Pallavi Aiyar

HARPER

First published in India by HarperCollins *Publishers* 2024
4th Floor, Tower A, Building No. 10, DLF Cyber City,
DLF Phase II, Gurugram, Haryana – 122002
www.harpercollins.co.in

4 6 8 10 9 7 5 3

P-ISBN: 978-93-5029-016-3
E-ISBN: 978-93-5029-247-1

Typeset in 11/15 Cambria at
SÜRYA

Printed and bound at
Replika Press Pvt.Ltd.

For Julio

CONTENTS

chapter one

SOYABEAN

Stalking Dragonflies

A beam of hot sun leaked through the leaves of the tree I was crouching under. My nose twitched. I badly needed to sneeze. But I forced myself to ignore the itch and focus on the prey in sight. Stalking was serious business after all. I held my crouch, frozen like a stone.

The buzzing of the dragonfly was deliciously exciting. I moved an inch closer and then another inch, until it was hovering directly above me, darting in and out of a bamboo thicket, totally unaware that I was so close. It was a perfect setup. I wanted to leap high, higher than I ever had before, up into the white sky and pluck it out of the air.

But just at the moment I was readying to launch, Ma's penetrating meow calling me back for a lunchtime feed and sent the dragonfly gliding away from my outstretched claws. In a flash it had disappeared over the grey brick walls of the courtyard.

I had been trying to catch a dragonfly from the time my eyes had opened. It was much harder than it sounded and no matter how silently I stalked or how quickly I jumped, I had always failed.

Ma told me to be patient. I was still too young she said.

But I felt that even though I was small, I was quick and talented and fierce and dragonflies should beware of me.

My belly rumbled. In the heat of the dragonfly chase I'd forgotten how late it was; definitely time for lunch. I began to trot back towards the corner of the covered corridor where Nai Nai had made a home of old cloth and cardboard for Ma and me. The more I thought of the creamy milk I would soon be slurping down, the faster I ran until I was bounding at full speed, the warm spring wind rushing past.

I was golden, like a tiger and full of energy and strength. I never felt tired and Ma had given up trying to get me to take an afternoon nap. There was so much to do and see and explore. I simply couldn't understand why anyone would waste their time sleeping.

I was the lone kitten in Ma's litter. I knew this was very unusual for us cats because we tended to have large families.

'Maomi! Little kitten!' Nai Nai would croon as she tickled me into wiggly delight.

'You are a model cat for the new China and your Ma a model citizen. Look at how she has obeyed the one-child policy and produced you; you Little Emperor cat; you very pretty maomi.'

Nai Nai was the oldest Ren, in the Xu household, the human family who owned the siheyuan we lived in. I worshipped her as did all the cats. In the evening when the rest of the family was busy gulping beer, cracking sunflower seeds and playing long, loud games of cards, Nai Nai would sneak away to be with us.

She would steal scraps of food from the kitchen to feed us, crunchy morsels of chicken feet and still-hot bits of fish skin. We would mill around her legs, rubbing our heads against her knobbly knees. I would then roll on my back, purring, cajoling her into tickling my tummy. Nai Nai's hands were dry and wrinkled but her touch was soft and her voice gentle.

She would spend hours talking to us, almost as if we were Ren. Ma explained to me that the real Ren in her life had disappointed her so often that she had come to prefer us cats.

I was Nai Nai's particular favourite. After she had finished stroking and feeding the other cats it was to the corner that Ma and I lived in that she came and sat.

'Lovely little maomi,' she would sigh as I burrowed into the crook of her arm.

Life was really quite good for a Little Emperor like me. I had Ma all to myself unlike some of my cousins who had to share their mothers with six or seven siblings. And even though I was an only kitten I never lacked for company. The courtyard we lived in was filled with aunts and uncles and cousins. There were black cats and white cats and golden, caramel-coloured cats like Ma and me.

Even Ba showed up once in a while. I would wake one morning and there he would be, his crooked smile sketched across his face. He always brought along an offering for us when he visited. A fish head he had scrounged out of the dustbins behind the restaurants that lined nearby Ghost Street or a choice, plump part of a bird he might have brought down.

Ba was a superb hunter. I wanted to be just like him when I grew up.

'Hmmm,' Ma would growl pursing her lips when I told her my feelings but I knew that deep down in her heart she admired Ba too. He was so handsome and dashing, it was impossible not to.

Our siheyuan was located in a hutong alleyway just off East Drum Tower Avenue. Although the paint was peeling from its walls, and the roof leaked when it rained, the yard was large and spacious and Nai Nai had filled it with pots and plants.

Outside the courtyard was the World. 'The Worrrrld!' Just the sound of the word was electrifying. It rolled roundly in the mouth, tasting of adventure.

The older cats of the courtyard spent hours every day wandering the World, making friends, besting foes and stalking prey. They would return with tales of long-whiskered rats and snub-nosed, Pekinese dogs that filled me with an almost unbearable curiosity.

But we kittens were kept confined to the yard. We weren't able yet to vault across the high walls of the siheyuan and our mothers liked to keep us close in any case. I wanted nothing more than to be grown up enough to go wandering with the adults and would beg to be allowed out with my older cousins.

'Patience, little one' Ma would say. The problem of course was that I didn't have any.

Nai Nai was also big on patience.

'Patience is a bitter plant, but it has sweet fruit,' she often told Xiao Xu, the grandson of the Xu family, but the young man would only laugh at her and call her old fashioned. Then Nai Nai's face would crumple up and she would suddenly look very old and very alone and would come to find us cats for company.

One evening the Xu family had friends over for dinner. From my little corner in the covered corridor I could hear much noisy laughter wafting out of the kitchen. The fizz of beer bottles being opened and the clink of glasses followed by shouts of, 'Gan bei! Bottoms up!' became louder and louder as the night wore on.

I was bursting with curiosity but when I tried to

make my way to the kitchen window to peek in, Ma extended her long paw and yanked me back.

'But why can't I look?' I whined.

'Don't ask so many questions,' she snapped.

I sulked, flattening my ears and hanging my head low. I hated being told what to do. Ma was always preventing me from doing anything remotely exciting. She was so very dull.

But I cheered up a few minutes later when I made out Nai Nai's bent figure emerging from the shadows of the main building. She walked slowly towards us. Too impatient to wait for her to reach me, I went leaping out to her, nipping her ankles in delight.

'Hello little maomi,' Nai Nai smiled as she scooped me up. But there was a flatness in her voice that even I knew meant she was unhappy, and that usually meant that she had argued with the family.

She carried me to the side of the yard opposite the kitchen and sat down resting her back against a pillar. The dinner party was still on in full swing although the voices of the Xus and their guests were increasingly slurred.

'Maomi, they dare to call themselves Chinese, this family of mine,' said Nai Nai with a sharpness that I wasn't used to in her. I wiggled around in her arms trying to make her smile but she was too distracted.

'All that is good in China and noble about being Chinese, they reject,' she continued. 'They laugh at the classics. The *Dream of the Red Chamber* is foolish they say and they call the great poet Du Fu boring! Peking Opera is too noisy for my grandson and even my son thinks calligraphy is a waste of time. I tell you, they are like a family of frogs sitting at the bottom of a well!'

'"Chinese need to be more practical Ma," my son says all puffed up with importance. He has the guts to condescend to me! His mother! "Calligraphy doesn't make money Ma; Poetry doesn't buy cars." But I ask you maomi, what is the use of money without poetry? What use is a fancy car when you lack a soul? Is practicality of more value than beauty?'

'Why have we Chinese lost our sense of wonder? Where is our dignity in this ocean of vulgarity, little kitten? I just don't know any more!'

'They don't read, they watch TV. They don't go to the theatre but to the disco. What with all this SMS and computers I wouldn't be surprised if Xiao Xu has forgotten how to write Chinese characters altogether!' Nai Nai raged on.

'How many times have I told him that the one who doesn't like to read is no better than the one who cannot read?'

By this time I had stopped wiggling and was paying attention to what she was saying.

'Oh little maomi, what would you know of the things I have seen? For you are a kitten of the shining, "New China". The world is all sunshine and play for Little Emperors like you.'

'But for me life's held different cards. How I have suffered from men and their endless wars and revolutions. Sometimes I feel I've been left with nothing: my youth, my hopes, they've all gone. It's not been easy maomi, not for any of us Chinese.'

Nai Nai held me up in front of her and looked straight into my eyes. I was fascinated, if confused by her words.

'So here I am little one, nearly eighty years old. A dead husband; my many children scattered to the wind. Except for Lao Xu, of course; my one surviving son. And then there's Xiao Xu . . .'

Nai Nai's voice trailed off in despair. It was already very late and the party in the kitchen appeared finally to be winding down. She gave me a last scratch under the chin and then rose to return to her bedroom for the night.

I knew why Nai Nai had been lost for words when it came to Xiao Xu. I was only a few days old when Ma had first warned me of this Ren.

'You be careful of that one,' she had meowed, indicating the podgy, spoilt, grandson of the family. 'That one has a knife in his belly.'

It was just as well that Ma had warned me of Xiao Xu. I knew to steer well clear of him but several of my cousins had had their tails yanked when they blundered too close to his hard, pinching hands. There was even a rumour that as a boy, the Xu grandson had set fire to the whiskers of a little kitten.

I was so frightened when I heard this that I went running to Ma to hide in the comfort of her fur. She had nuzzled me lightly and told me not to worry. Nai Nai would never let anything bad happen to us, she had said.

But although I was usually very brave and unafraid of even the biggest dragonfly, I couldn't help feeling a shiver of fear whenever Xiao Xu happened to be around. There was something disturbing in the way he smiled when he looked at me, as if he didn't really mean the smile. There was no kindness in his eyes at all.

I wasn't very clear what exactly he did. Lao Xu, his father, was an official at the Public Security Bureau, which I knew was a grand and important job. Every day many Ren came to the house to ask Lao Xu for favours of different kinds.

He was obviously very helpful because the Ren usually brought along briefcases full of presents for him. I was always excited when these presents arrived because sometimes they included gifts of fine food, scraps of which could, were I lucky, end up in my tummy. But, Nai Nai greeted these visitors and their briefcases with a stony face.

'Maomi,' she once said to me. 'Don't you think its better to like what you have than have what you like?' This was quite a complicated thought and it made my head spin, but I had the feeling it was a good thought nonetheless.

Xiao Xu sat with his father when the visitors came but when Lao Xu was away at work, the young man spent most of the day lounging around the house, eating peanuts and talking on his mobile phone. I didn't understand much of his endless phone conversations. He was always referring to 'real estate' and 'deals' and most of all to 'money'.

I knew 'money' was something that was very important to Ren or at least to most Ren. Nai Nai was the only one who didn't seem to care much about it.

'What is the value of money when it can so easily be used up?' I heard her ask Xiao Xu.

'Learning can never be used up. Wisdom is never depleted. Fill your head rather than your pocket and you can never be robbed.'

Xiao Xu merely sneered at her, smiling that unkind smile I found so chilling.

The dusty, warm spring days slipped by so quickly that the scorching summer had arrived before I knew it. I grew bigger and stronger although I still hadn't caught a dragonfly and I still couldn't leap over the courtyard walls and I still didn't have the patience Ma kept urging me to get.

Then one day I saw Nai Nai coming out of the main pavilion and from the way she was walking, I immediately knew that something was wrong. Tears floated in her eyes although she was smiling in a funny, determined way.

Ma must have noticed too because she began to stiffen and arch her back as though preparing to scare something bad away.

Nai Nai knelt in front of Ma and me and began to scratch me under the chin in just the way she knew I liked best.

'Maomi,' she said after a few minutes, 'you must be brave now, agreed?'

I felt filled with importance. Nai Nai had come to the right kitten if she was looking for bravery. I was without doubt the bravest kitten in the yard. I would be willing to take on a rat double my size if need be, especially if Nai Nai wanted me to.

I meowed impatiently wanting Nai Nai to explain what she needed from me. Although I didn't want to admit it, I hoped it wasn't a dragonfly because I still wasn't very good at stalking them.

'I have some good news,' she continued, her smile so fixed it looked like it was glued on to her face.

'I just got a call from a friend who lives in a nearby hutong and she says she knows two waiguo ren, foreigners, who are looking to take in a kitten.'

I didn't quite understand what any of this had to do with me but I could hear Ma's breathing becoming faster and more uneven. I began to feel a little nervous. Both Nai Nai and Ma were looking at me very peculiarly.

'Maomi, don't be afraid,' said Nai Nai. 'The foreigners live in a courtyard not far from here and

I will come and see you whenever I can. You'll have a good home with them little kitten. I know they are not Chinese and don't know our ways but how does that matter? You will learn theirs.'

It slowly began to dawn on me that Nai Nai was planning to send me away to go and live with these two, strange, waiguo Ren; far away from home, far away from my cousins and aunts and uncles and worst of all, far away from Ma.

I began to struggle against Nai Nai in panic. I wanted to run and hide where no waiguo Ren could find me, but she held on to me firmly.

'Now listen maomi,' she commanded. 'The foreigners may look peculiar but they will feed you well and pamper you. I've heard that they buy their pets very expensive, special food that comes in tins and even make special homes and clothes and toys for them.

'You'll be better off with them, trust me, little kitten. They will treat you like the Little Emperor you are.'

'Who was that on the phone, just now?' demanded Xiao Xu roughly, interrupting Nai Nai.

He marched up to us and snatched me out of his grandmother's hands.

'Is it true that some foreigners actually want this . . .' he paused to look at me before going on, 'useless creature?'

I was quaking in his hands from fright and pain.

His grip was too tight. Ma began to pace up and down, between his legs restlessly, meowing up at him in distress. Xiao Xu kicked her hard in the ribs.

'Shut up you stupid cat,' he snapped before turning to Nai Nai.

'Are they going to pay? Did you ask them how much they would be willing to give?' he said excitedly.

Nai Nai's eyes flashed angrily and she pulled herself up tall. Suddenly she didn't look old or wrinkled but strong and fierce.

'Give the kitten back to me, now,' she growled and in one, smooth motion freed me from Xiao Xu's clutch. 'Yes, the foreigners will pay,' she continued. 'They will pay with their time and love and willingness to look after this maomi. And that is more than we can ask from anyone young man. Can you understand that?'

Xiao Xu seemed a little taken aback by Nai Nai's ferocity.

'Relax Nai Nai,' he laughed nervously. 'I was just asking because you're not familiar with the ways of the world. Foreigners have a lot of money you see, which they're willing to part with for the stupidest things. Like this kitten, for example!'

'They come to our country and make good business here. Why shouldn't we Chinese profit from them too? Do they want an apartment, these foreign friends of yours, Nai Nai? Perhaps a grand courtyard house? I can help them, you know. I have friends in high places. Foreigners need local Chinese assistance, after all. It's easy for them to get ripped off otherwise.'

Xiao Xu chuckled nastily as if he had made a very funny joke. 'Come on Nai Nai,' he said. 'Let's deliver this little maomi of yours to the waiguo ren. I'll drive you.'

I looked desperately for Ma. She had picked herself up from where she'd fallen when Xiao Xu had kicked her. She was looking straight at me, her golden eyes, deep pools of love. I wanted to look into her eyes forever. My heart was hurting and racing at the same time.

'Man zou,' Ma meowed softly, 'go slowly little one,' and then she turned her face away.

chapter two

TOFU

The Dustbin

I was born into a world made orange with grit. Flecks of sand snuck into my mouth as I sucked and pulled on Mama's teat but I was so hungry I didn't much mind. Beijing, in April, could be a hostile city with screaming winds carrying in hundreds of tons of hot-cold earth from far away deserts.

But the rusted walls of the garbage can we lived in provided some shelter and it was easy to forget about the dust and wind when snuggled against Mama's always-warm belly.

There were five of us siblings. Mama named us according to the order in which we were born. So I was Number Three, the only girl in the litter.

Number One was the boss, our Da Ge or big brother. He was the largest amongst us and the tawny streaks in his otherwise black fur shone especially bright. He always got first pick of Mama's teats and belched the loudest after a feed. Number Two, was envious of Da Ge's burps but try as he did to match them he never did manage, neither in strength nor smell.

I was twenty days old before I managed to pluck up the courage to clamber out of the garbage can and into the open World. My brothers had already been out the day before and had spent the night meowing excitedly about the colours, scents and shapes of what they had seen until Mama swatted them into silence.

The garbage can smelt of damp fur, mould and Mama. I liked the smell. The main colours I had seen were the black and brown of my family. I liked these colours. Although interested in the new shapes and sights the others were so enchanted by, I couldn't help being nervous at the prospect of so much newness.

'I don't mind staying behind,' I said. But Da Ge was insistent that I see for myself.

The next day we woke early and he wetly nosed me from behind, nudging me all the way out of the garbage can and onto the cracked earth of the college campus on which our dustbin-home was located. I was terrified at the limitlessness of the World. I looked up into the grey morning sky and blinked.

Number Two and Number Five were tumbling around besides us, blurs of energy. Number Four was off mewling somewhere but I could barely hear him, my ears too full with the big sounds of the outside.

There were whirrs and whistles, roars and ringing. Mama had told me a little about the things the sounds belonged to: machines called cars and bicycles, lawn mowers and mobile phones. And the machines in turn belonged to Ren.

Ren was a complex category and I wasn't quite sure what to make of it. From what Mama told me, Ren could be wise and ignorant, cruel and tolerant. They could love us cats, scratching us behind the ears for long purr-filled minutes.

But some Ren were dangerous. I felt a spasm of fear as I recalled the tightness in Mama's voice when she told us that there were even Ren who liked to eat us.

'We are dustbin cats,' Mama had said flatly almost as soon as we were born. 'And the World is not an easy place for us. We must spend our lives swallowing wind and eating bitterness. Find food where we can. Forage in dustbins and other dark, smelly places where Ren discard what they no longer want, yet seem to resent our taking it.'

The sourness on her breath when she spoke of such matters chilled my tummy no matter how close I snuggled against the warmth of my brothers. I couldn't bear the hardness of her expression sometimes but there was nothing I could do to soften it.

Mama wasn't always like that. In the mornings she was gentle and her eyes would shine as she watched us slurp up her milk. But then she would leave to look for food and when she returned many hours later, her eyes were tired and faded. Sometimes she tried to ignore us as we rushed to her, but our exuberance was impossible to fight and she would eventually lie down on her side in surrender so we could feed.

She rarely spoke about her daily outings scrounging for scraps although she often cautioned us about trusting Ren and I knew there were things in her past that she hid from us. The secrets were stamped on her body.

Places where her fur was burnt off and never grew back; the missing tip of an ear; the slight limp with which she walked. She didn't offer explanations for these things and somehow we knew not to ask. Mama might have been a dustbin cat but she was very proud.

A few nights before my first visit to the World, Mama had returned to the garbage can earlier than usual. Her normally strained expression was absent and she looked almost happy. She played with us, ruffling our fur softly with her paws and tickling our faces with her whiskers as we skidded around trying to latch on to her nipples.

After we had eaten our tummies into tight drums, she allowed us to press up close to her. She gazed at us with a tight look and I wasn't sure if it was love or pain that I saw in it.

'Soon you will grow up and leave me,' she sighed, a declaration that prompted many squeaks of protest to the contrary.

'No! Listen to me children,' she said with an urgency that shushed us into stillness.

'Wherever life takes you, you must always remember that while you might have been born in a dustbin, you are not of dustbin stock.'

Sensing a story we settled ourselves to listen, our newly-opened eyes wide with curiosity, but Mama suddenly changed the topic.

'Old Man Zhao is one of the good Ren. He fed me a juicy piece of liver today,' she said.

Mama often spoke of Old Man Zhao, a Ren who was kind to her and had allowed her to make her home in the garbage can in the yard behind his apartment.

We were usually quite interested in hearing stories about Old Man Zhao, but not on that evening. Mama's mention of the fact that we were not of dustbin stock sounded far more exciting and we pressed her to return to that tale.

Old Man Zhao's piece of liver obviously had her in an indulgent mood that night and instead of reminding us that it was past our bedtime, she relented and began to speak.

'It might be difficult for you to believe children,

but your great great great grandfather, the fabulously fat Fei Fei, used to have his supper served to him on silver plates. On occasion he'd be offered upto seventy courses in a single evening, great steaming dishes of fatty pork and lightly-spiced beef, succulent rabbit ears and nutritious bullfrog's ovaries.'

My mouth had begun to overflow just listening to this description and by the wet feel of drool descending down my head I knew that Number Four who was resting his chin on it, was feeling much the same.

'You see Fei Fei was the favourite pet of a very wealthy and powerful Ren, a Manchu nobleman who ordered that the cat be fed with ivory chopsticks by a servant whose sole duty was to ensure that his porcelain bowl and jade water cup were never empty,' said Mama.

I felt my eyes grow so big that they felt like bursting. Jade! Ivory! Such strange and beautiful words!

Over the next few days we pestered Mama every chance we got to tell us more about Fei Fei. I liked to hear about him mostly because it seemed to put Mama in a good mood. Her usually tired eyes sparkled when talking about our fancy, well-fed ancestor.

One thing puzzled me though. How was it that if our ancestor was rich and pampered, we ourselves had fallen on such hard times. When I asked Mama, she shook her head.

'It's very complicated, little Number Three,' she said. 'Fortunes change in China faster than even the fastest cat can run. History has left so many in this country bereft.'

'What's "bereft"?' I whispered to Da Ge who was nearby.

He seemed not to hear me but I thought he was only pretending because he didn't like to admit there were things even he didn't know.

Meanwhile, Mama continued to talk.

'My Nai Nai, your great grandmother had a master who was a rich merchant trading silks and tea. But then there was a communist revolution and suddenly the World became a bad place for wealthy Ren. The merchant had everything taken away from him by the new government and soon afterwards he disappeared with his family. But my Nai Nai was left behind with nowhere to go to except the dustbins.

'And so children,' Mama meowed sadly, 'our family finds itself in this poor situation today. She paused and looked at us in silence before giving me a quick lick on the head.

'But don't have heavy hearts. If ever life gets you down remember that we are of noble stock and conduct yourself with pride and dignity.'

Mama's words were ringing in my ears that first day that I ventured out into the World. It was a big day for me and I desperately wanted to do her proud by being dignified. This wasn't very easy because my fur was coarse and patchy. I had scratched bits of it off when the fleas became really unbearable.

And I also felt so small compared to the bigness of everything out there in the open. I had never been outside the dustbin before and I missed the smell of Mama already. But I was trying my best, holding my head high and my back straight with a confidence I didn't really feel.

I was especially keen to make a good impression on Old Man Zhao when we met because he had been so caring towards Mama. I wanted him to like me and to know I was grateful to him. At the same time though, I couldn't help being a little scared at the thought of actually meeting a Ren. Mama had so often said they were unpredictable.

Could any Ren really be trusted? Even a kind one?

Da Ge and my other brothers had already seen Old Man Zhao the day before when I had stayed behind in the dustbin.

'He's very handsome,' Number Two told me that night.

I wondered how he could tell. After all, Old Man Zhao was the very first Ren he had ever seen.

Now as I tottered around behind Da Ge, Number Two came bounding up to us. 'Come and see Old Man Zhao,' he meowed breathlessly. 'The Ren is out at the front.'

Our dustbin sat on the hard, neglected earth to the back of Old Man Zhao's ground-floor apartment. But the front of the house had a tidy little garden. As we followed Number Two around to it, I felt my heartbeat quicken.

We turned the corner and all of a sudden there he was; the most curious, most wonderful creature I had ever seen.

Old Man Zhao!

He had shiny, white hair on his head but his body was hairless; his brown skin covered in something I later discovered was called 'clothes'. I drank it all in. No paws, no whiskers, no tail. This was definitely not a cat. It was in fact a real Ren!

My teeth chattered with excitement and my tail brushed the floor in wide, sweeping motions.

Old Man Zhao's eyes were half closed as though he was looking at something inside himself. And he was moving his body in a peculiar way, so quietly it was like he wasn't moving at all. He slowly extended his arms and bent his knees, turning this way and that.

That evening Mama told me that what I had seen was called Tai Chi. It was a kind of exercise that Ren liked.

I was fascinated. There was so much about Ren I still had to learn. I wondered if there was some way to learn about Ren without actually being with them. That would really be perfect I thought, because although I was interested in them, Ren were so different from cats, they frightened me a little.

Not Old Man Zhao, though.

That first day when his Tai Chi exercise was over and he opened his eyes up fully, Old Man Zhao saw all five of us siblings sitting in a row staring up at him. I suddenly felt very shy and tried to retreat to escape his gaze.

But there was nowhere immediate to hide and I knew Mama liked him. So although ready to run if necessary, I stayed put.

Old Man Zhao looked at us for a long, still moment. Then he turned around and went into his house. My brothers and I were at a loss. But before we could decide on our next move, the Ren was coming back out of the apartment. He walked up to a spot near us and set down two bowls of milk.

Da Ge and Number Two immediately leapt forward towards the bowls, but I held back.

Was it a trap? Would this Ren lure us in with milk and then hurt us? These were the questions racing in my mind.

But then Old Man Zhao turned around and returned to his home. I saw my older bothers lapping away at the milk and when even Number Four and Number Five joined them, I finally threw caution to the wind and went running up to get my share.

We ate so much that our tummies touched the ground and we could barely move. We must have looked comical as we flopped around the garden trying to play but too sleepy to have much energy. Later, I noticed Old Man Zhao peering out at us from behind a curtain, a half-smile on his lips.

He was like that, Old Man Zhao. We never saw much of him but he was always so nice, leaving out little treats for us to eat and also toys to play with. On some days we would find a ball of wool waiting for us at his apartment's doorstep; on others, a plastic mouse or a piece of old cloth.

As we tore around the garden, tumbling over each other to get at these treasures, Old Man Zhao would watch from a distance, his eyes creased up in amusement.

The Old Man was almost always alone. The neighbours who lived in the apartments above his rarely spoke to him. At most they gave him a small nod as they brushed past him on their way up the stairs.

Most evenings he would sit on his doorstep reading a book. But sometimes he would put on music, throw open the windows and come out into the garden to dance. It was a slow, elegant dance that Mama told me was called a Waltz. She said the Waltz was normally danced with two Ren holding each other. But Old Man Zhao's wife had died many years ago and so he danced empty armed.

Mama said there had been a time when the Old Man had been a very famous professor at the college. But then a book he wrote made some powerful Ren angry and for a long time he wasn't allowed to teach any classes at all. Now he was too old to teach in any case and it seemed as if everyone had forgotten about him.

I asked Mama about what was in the book he'd written that had made the others so upset, but she didn't know. 'Ren are as the wind. Who can say why they blow this way or that?' she shrugged.

As far as I could tell there was only one Ren who regularly came to visit Old Man Zhao. Her name was Madam Wang and whenever I saw her walking briskly up to his apartment, I scrambled to find something to hide behind. She had never been unkind to any of us but I had heard enough about her to make me quite terrified.

Madam Wang was in fact very famous amongst the cats on the university campus. We knew she ran what she called a 'cat protection society,' but from what I could make out she didn't do much protection at all.

Instead she was known for taking away little kittens from their mothers and poking them with needles and putting stinging drops of liquid in their eyes. Sometimes she returned the kittens to their families but sometimes they were never seen again.

Our litter had avoided these horrors so far, but I could see her eyes weighing us up every time she came to visit Old Man Zhao.

One morning we were out playing in the garden scuttling in and out of Old Man Zhao's legs making it as difficult as possible for him to focus on his Tai Chi exercises.

'Chi fan le ma? Have you eaten?' called out Madam Wang announcing her presence with the traditional greeting.

'Yes, I've eaten,' replied Old Man Zhao in the correct

manner, straightening up his knees from their bent, Tai Chi position. 'What can I do for you?'

Madam Wang turned her slanting, black eyes at us. 'How are the cats?' she asked.

'Well, they're kittens. They play. They're no bother,' said the Old Man cautiously.

'No bother, *yet*,' Madam Wang corrected him sharply.

'Soon, they'll grow bigger and hungrier and you won't be able to afford to feed them. Not on your pension. And what will you do when they start having babies?'

Old Man Zhao stared back at her in silence.

'We have to find them homes,' said Madam Wang decisively.

I began to feel quite peculiar. What did she mean? We already had a home.

Old Man Zhao and Madam Wang disappeared into the apartment leaving us kittens to ourselves. I turned my head this way and that trying to see if any of my brothers could explain what Madam Wang had said. But they all looked equally unsure.

That day none of us were in the mood to play much. I just wanted the time to pass as quickly as possible so that I could see Mama again and cuddle up to her and have her tell me that everything would be well.

Finally, it was evening and Mama returned home to the dustbin. We surrounded her, all meowing at the same time so that she couldn't understand anything. When we quietened down, she asked Da

Ge to explain what we were going on about. He recounted the day's events and what Madam Wang had said to Old Man Zhao that morning.

'What did she mean Mama?' I asked urgently, my voice squeaky with anxiety.

Mama just looked at all of us with tired eyes. 'Go to sleep children,' she finally said and turned her back.

I spent the next week trying to fight off a feeling of dread that refused to go away. Something was horribly wrong. Mama seemed to be becoming more and more cold towards us. There were no bedtime stories anymore and she wouldn't let us spend more than a minute or two on her teats. She acted almost as though she were in pain but there was no hurt on her body.

Then late one afternoon, just as the day was turning cooler, we saw Madam Wang again. This time she had two other Ren, a man and a woman, with her and what amazing Ren they were. I had never even imagined anything like them was possible.

The man was tall, with skin so white it hurt to look at him. His eyes were yellow-green like a cat's. But the woman was short and dark with round black eyes and a big, curvy nose.

'Run! Hide!' growled Da Ge. 'Now!'

I ran so fast I could hardly breathe. My brothers were besides me. We made our way to the back and clambered into the dustbin, panting. We tried to be as silent as possible and when after a few minutes nothing had happened, a wild hope surged up in me.

Perhaps it wasn't us that Madam Wang and the two strangers had come for. Or perhaps Old Man Zhao wouldn't tell them where to find us.

But then the darkening sky above our dustbin was blotted out as the faces of Old Man Zhao, Madam Wang and both strangers peered in, their eyes searching us out. I curled up into a tight little ball against my brother's panting bodies. I wanted so much to just disappear.

'Which one is the mu mao, the she-cat?' the dark Ren asked, turning to Old Man Zhao.

The next thing I knew hands were reaching inside the dustbin and plucking me up, away from my brothers. Da Ge bared his fangs and growled as threateningly as he could, but he was only a kitten and his teeth were small and his growl not very frightening at all.

The dark Ren was holding me away from her body and looking directly at my face. I twisted and struggled against her but she held on.

'Hello, little cat!' she said, smiling. 'What a pretty one you are. I'm going to call you Tofu.'

Madam Wang clapped her hands in excitement. "Tofu! That's a great name. Maomi,' she said 'your yunqi is very good.'

I knew that yunqi meant luck but how could she think I was lucky? As the two strange Ren carried me away, I felt I was the unluckiest cat in the world.

chapter three

SOYABEAN

Egg Yolk and Chicken Liver

The smell of boiling chicken liver pulled me towards the kitchen. Food was the most exciting thing in the world, I thought.

'Come on!' I meowed out to Tofu, 'it's liver for lunch.' But she was resting on the branches of the pomegranate tree with her face turned towards the sky and didn't reply.

She was a funny one, Tofu was. Always off dreaming.

I felt a bit guilty because she was so skinny. But even though I'd tried a few times to get her to eat more, she was just not that interested in food. So, most days I ate her meals too.

Nai Nai had been right. It really was the life being the pets of waiguo Ren. We got to eat egg yolk and yoghurt and liver and fish. Mrs A was always buying little treats of beef and chicken giblets for us. It was heaven.

I padded across the courtyard to the kitchen. Auntie Li gave me a sour look. She didn't like having to cook for us cats even when Mrs A gave her clear orders to. 'Catch a rat, you lazy good-for-nothing,' she'd say, prodding me with the broom that was never far away from her.

But although she fussed and muttered, in the end she would spoon out the food into our bowls.

Auntie may not have believed it but I was actually always on the look out for a rat to catch. I'd have made mincemeat of one, given half a chance. But there were none around.

The siheyuan was a bit dull like that. The World outside remained a secret. I tried to sneak out through the red doors of the courtyard's entrance whenever I had a chance but Mrs A always noticed and dragged me right back in. I suppose it didn't help being bright orange. I was very easy to spot.

And so apart from nipping at Auntie Li's broom while she swept the floors, there wasn't anything much exciting to do. The way Auntie flapped her arms as she tried to chase me down was funny, though.

Of course I was too quick for her.

Sometimes I was also able to get Tofu to come down the tree and play catch. She was a different kettle of fish to Auntie, so fast that even I had difficulty keeping up. Not that I'd have admitted this to her.

She hero-worshipped me because I was bigger and braver. I had looked after her from the day she was brought here by Mr and Mrs A. She was the smallest kitten imaginable but with such large, round eyes.

I had walked up to her, curious, as she'd lain curled tightly on a sweater Mrs A had put out. A second later, I was hopping around, howling with pain. Small though she was, Tofu had given my sniffing nose a stinging bite.

It was amazing how much it had hurt considering that she didn't have many teeth back then. But she was fierce when it came to defending herself and her soft snarls warned me from getting too close again.

Later I found out that she had been born in a dustbin which explained a lot. Like the way she took ages to trust anyone, cat or Ren. Or the way she preferred to sleep in a cold corner of the yard rather than on Mr and Mrs A's soft bed. Or the expression in her eyes, both sad and savage, when caught up in her thoughts.

That first night after all the Ren had gone to bed I'd heard her crying. In the beginning, I'd tried to ignore the sounds because I was still sulking at having had my nose bitten. But after a while I hadn't been able to bear hearing her so unhappy.

I'd found her hiding behind a chest of drawers in the living room; her fur damp with tears.

Not knowing what to say I'd just snuggled up next to her and after a while her cries had quietened down into sniffles. When she'd stopped shaking I'd touched her cautiously with my paw. That time she didn't bite.

'Don't cry,' I'd told her. 'Nai Nai said we must be brave and brave cats don't cry.'

Not that Nai Nai always followed her own advice because her eyes had been full of tears when she was dropping me off at the As' siheyuan. Xiao Xu had driven us here but he hadn't even glanced my way being too busy handing out his name cards to my new owners.

'Call me if any of your waiguo ren friends need to find a house in Beijing. I'll find you the best price,' he'd said.

Only then had he turned to me and patted my head half-heartedly as I squirmed in Nai Nai's arms.

'After all now that you are adopting our maomi, you are almost like family.'

He had flashed them the smile that wasn't really a smile, but I don't think Mr and Mrs A realized and they'd simply grinned back. Nai Nai had looked even more miserable than before though, and she'd abruptly handed me over to my new mistress.

I will never forget the moment Nai Nai disappeared through the doors of the courtyard. I'd felt I was being swallowed up by fright. I'd struggled out of Mrs A's hold and scampered away to hide behind a flower pot determined never to come out again until Nai Nai returned to fetch me.

But then later in the afternoon I'd heard Mrs A calling out for me. 'Come Soyabean, Lai!,' she'd said.

And so I'd learnt that I had a name. Not just maomi, but Soyabean.

Mrs A was holding out a bowl with some egg yolk and yoghurt, foods I'd never eaten before. I was both very hungry and very scared but in the end my stomach had won out and I'd emerged from my hiding place to eat.

Tofu joined us in the courtyard a week or so later. I had already settled in well by then but it was even nicer to have a sidekick around. And luckily she didn't eat too much so I could chomp up her leftovers as well.

After that first night we spent huddled together behind the chest of drawers, she began to follow me around everywhere. She admired me a lot because she was a very small cat; maybe two or three weeks younger than me. And she didn't know how to do many things. In the beginning, it was difficult for her even to climb up the few steps that led into the main living area. But luckily for her I was big and strong and could teach her everything.

I had to help her talk with Ren. I'd had loads of practice with Nai Nai and the other Xus but apart from someone called Old Man Zhao, Tofu had had almost no contact with them.

Ren were not the cleverest of creatures and they found it very hard to understand things. I had to explain to Tofu that simply crooking an ear or pointing a tail was not enough to communicate with them. They just weren't as smart as cats.

Instead, you had to meow a lot to get their attention. And the louder you meowed the quicker they responded. Tofu was never able to meow as loudly as I could and sometimes I had to help her out by meowing on her behalf.

She was a bit annoying like that; always getting locked in cupboards and drawers but unable to call out for help. The soft little 'eek' sounds she made couldn't even properly be called meows. It was then upto me to attract the attention of a Ren and get them to let Tofu out from wherever she was stuck.

The days in the new siheyuan sped by and soon it was late summer. White, bright clouds smudged the burning sky but brought no relief from the heat. I wished I could take off my fur like Ren took off their clothes.

Tofu and I spent the long afternoons sleeping at the foot of the pomegranate tree in the yard and even the droning of dragonflies wasn't enough to get us moving. Auntie Li would sometimes whack us with her broom if she caught us napping but we'd pretend not to notice and keep our eyes tightly shut until she'd wandered off to sweep somewhere else.

The courtyard had to be kept spotlessly clean because Ren were always coming by. Mr and Mrs A were very popular and had many friends both waiguo Ren and Chinese.

I hadn't realized how many different kinds of Ren there were. Just like cats. There were black Ren like Tofu and yellower ones like me and pinkish-white ones.

They would gather in the evening when it was cooler but still light and drink out of tall glasses and eat foreign Ren food. Tofu usually went off to hide when new Ren were around but I found them all quite interesting. And because I was golden and handsome most Ren would scratch me under the chin and say how good looking I was.

Mrs A always looked so proud when her friends praised me and sometimes she'd give me a quick kiss on the nose. But Mr A would scold her if he saw this. He said kissing cats was unhygienic. I didn't understand what that meant but was sure it couldn't be true, whatever it was.

One day Mrs A came looking for me, a grin darting across her face. She looked very pretty and I felt proud to be her cat. 'Soyabean,' she said tickling my ears, 'we have a surprise for you this evening.'

I was very curious. What could it be? Some new kind of food? That would be exciting although some things foreigners ate weren't that great. I'd tried a slimy green thing called an 'olive' the other day. It was pretty disgusting. It wasn't polite to hurt the As' feelings though and I always tried my best to eat up whatever they offered, (even though I'd buried the olive under the pomegranate tree when Mrs A wasn't looking).

'You'll be having special visitors tonight, Soyabean. I better have you brushed to smarten you up,' Mrs A continued.

Visitors for me? Who? I really couldn't imagine. My wondering was cut short by Auntie Li who on Mrs A's orders began to attack me with a poky brush. At first I was quite indignant because I felt I was already smart enough and didn't really need the grooming. But the more I protested the more energetically Auntie Li brushed. So in the end I gave up and allowed her to finish without a struggle.

That evening I went leaping to the door the moment someone knocked. But it was only Mr J, one of Mr A's waiguo Ren friends. I'd met this one before. He was nice enough, always quick to stroke me and say what a handsome cat I was.

But while normally I would have been happy to see him, today I couldn't help being disappointed. Surely Mr J couldn't be the special visitor Mrs A had promised?

Just then there was another knock. Mr A opened the doors and I almost stopped breathing.

There stood Nai Nai as though she had never gone away. She looked exactly the same, her kind eyes soft with laughter and her wrinkled hands held out for me to jump into.

'Look who's come to see you Soyabean,' said Mr A but before he'd even finished the sentence I was in Nai Nai's arms, purring louder than a lion's roar.

'Ai ya! Maomi!' murmured Nai Nai burying her face in my fur. 'How big you've grown and how fine!'

'I see they've been feeding you well, your waiguo ren owners, maomi,' Xiao Xu suddenly loomed up behind Nai Nai. 'Getting quite plump,' he said poking me roughly with his finger.

I shrank deeper into Nai Nai's arms as he brushed past her into the courtyard.

'Well, well! This is certainly the life!'

The neat yard with its pomegranate tree and bamboo garden furniture twinkled in the light thrown up by the spicy scented candles Mrs A had lit.

'Do come in and sit down,' Mr A urged Nai Nai and Xiao Xu.

Mr J was already relaxing on one of the chairs with a drink in hand. I really wanted Tofu to meet Nai Nai but of course she was nowhere to be seen. She was such a scaredy cat.

'Xie! Xie! Thank you for looking after this maomi so well,' Nai Nai's voice choked as she took Mrs A's hands in hers.

'Madam Xu, it's us who should thank you for giving Soyabean to us,' replied Mrs A warmly. 'He's been such a precious gift. I simply couldn't imagine life without him and Tofu.'

'Who's Tofu?' interrupted Xiao Xu, a sneer playing on his lips. 'Not another cat!' 'How much money do you waiguo ren have? How much do you spend on food for two spoilt cats every month?'

'Xiao Xu!' said Nai Nai sharply. 'Hold your tongue. Such talk makes us lose face. Our waiguo friends have honoured us with an invitation to their home and all you can talk about is money! What will they think?'

'It's quite alright Madam Xu,' said Mrs A quickly. 'I don't mind in the least. Xiao Xu is right. Pets aren't cheap. But Soyabean and Tofu give us so much joy. There's no price tag to that is there?'

'You sound just like Nai Nai, Mrs A,' giggled Xiao Xu. 'In fact, everything has a price tag! Women can be so sentimental as I'm sure your husband will agree,' he continued giving Mr A an exaggerated wink.

Mrs A looked angry though not as angry as Nai Nai who was shaking with rage. I was right by her feet, so I could tell.

'It's a beautiful evening,' interrupted Mr J, who had been quietly sipping his drink until then.

I thought this was a bit of a strange thing to say but Ren did seem to like talking about the weather. When it rained they would say, 'It's raining!' even though it was quite obvious that it was.

They liked to waste words, these Ren. A cat only meowed when necessary. This was a big difference between us. Something I had to explain to Tofu many times.

As the evening wore on I stuck by Nai Nai's side. She was silent for most of the time, stroking me steadily while the others talked and only ate small bites of food. Tofu remained vanished, though once I saw her creeping about in the far corner of the yard.

My eyelids were getting quite droopy when dinner was over, Mr J got up to say goodbye. 'Thank you so much,' he said shaking Mrs A's hand.

'You're very welcome,' she replied. 'We'll be sorry to see you leave Beijing.'

Was Mr J leaving Beijing? Why? I tried to make an effort to concentrate but I was so sleepy I had to force my eyes to stay open.

'It's going to be rather serious, this virus,' Mr J said gravely. 'It's your choice to stay put of course but I would consider it carefully. If the city is quarantined you'll be stuck. It'll be too late to get out then.'

What virus? What was 'quarantined'? I didn't follow what was being said at all. It made my head spin.

'You waiguo ren are always so quick to believe the worst about China,' snarled Xiao Xu suddenly, 'and so scared of everything. Mr A you are absolutely right to stay on in Beijing. You really mustn't believe a word of the lies the foreign media are always spreading.'

Xiao Xu looked slyly at Nai Nai, 'After all, the truth must take the straight road while lies travel on the wind.'

This was something I'd heard Nai Nai tell Xiao Xu a hundred times and he had always just laughed at

her in response. It was strange to hear him talk now as though he had thought up of the words all on his own.

'Look, I don't want to upset you,' Mr J said throwing up his hands. 'And you're welcome not to believe the foreign papers. But your government hasn't exactly got a great history of truth-telling, has it?'

There was a silence in which the two Ren glared at each other. But then Mr J turned his back on Xiao Xu and came towards me.

'Anyway, you come here Soyabean,' he said scooping me up into a hug and breaking the silence. 'What a gorgeous, gorgeous cat you are. All golden and shiny.' I began to purr with pleasure and even forgave Auntie Li for the hard brushing she'd given me earlier. The compliments had made it worth it.

'Mr A,' continued Mr J, 'you're sitting on a goldmine here. This Soyabean of yours should be a cat model. You could make millions off him. He's simply perfect! Can you imagine him running towards a bowl of cat food, all glowing and fluffy? No one would be able to resist him!'

Everyone chuckled and talk of the virus ended.

But I noticed Xiao Xu staring at me in a very peculiar way. I didn't like it at all and even though it was a warm night my ears felt cold.

'Well, thank you both very much but we should be leaving as well,' Nai Nai said getting to her feet, once the chatter had died down.

'So soon? Are you well Madam Xu?' asked Mrs A. 'You look a little uncomfortable.'

'Please don't worry. I'm very well,' replied Nai Nai. 'With gracious hosts like you, how could I be otherwise?' She sighed.

'I just worry about this maomi sometimes. It's not the Chinese way to praise the ones we love so openly. It only attracts the evil eye.'

Xiao Xu let out a loud groan. 'Ai! This Nai Nai of mine is so superstitious. You must forgive her. She's old. Why shouldn't the maomi be praised? Your friend is correct Mr A. This Soyabean of yours hasn't turned out bad looking at all. Strange, considering how ugly his bony mother is, but then you must feed him on the finest meats.'

Mrs A gave Xiao Xu a thin-lipped smile. 'Well, my Soyabean is certainly a lovely cat.' She turned to Nai Nai, 'And Madam Xu, I really must thank you again for having brought him to us. Do come and visit anytime you like. Soyabean will be thrilled to see you.'

Late that night when everyone had finally left and the Ren had gone to sleep, Tofu emerged at last. She came up and lay down beside me. It was muggy and still. In the moonlight her eyes looked larger than ever.

'Your Nai Nai is nice,' she said after a while, 'kind, like Old Man Zhao. But there's something very wrong with that Xiao Xu.'

chapter four

TOFU

The Warning

Soyabean couldn't sit still for a single moment; he was so excited about becoming a model. Not that he'd ever been particularly still even before the big news.

I didn't know much about modelling but it didn't sound very nice. I imagined it would involve being around many strange Ren. I thought that I would rather go back to being a dustbin cat than become a model.

Or maybe that wasn't true. When I remembered the empty look in Mama's eyes after she returned home in the evenings, limping with exhaustion, I knew that perhaps there was nothing worse than being a dustbin cat. Spending your whole life hungry and cold and wet, with fleas deep in your fur eating away at you.

I understood now what Madam Wang had meant by my yunqi being good. I really was a very lucky cat. Mr and Mrs A were the most wonderful Ren that existed. They were patient and gentle with me even though I wasn't very good at communicating with them.

And there was always so much to eat in the house that I could never manage to finish my share. Soyabean would then gobble it up and I let him because it made him so happy and in any case my stomach just wasn't used to being totally full.

Soyabean was very special to me. Those first few days in the courtyard when everything was strange and new, he was the one that used to curl up with me at night and tell me not to cry.

I missed Mama very much but having Soyabean by my side made it more bearable. And he helped me slowly to understand the Ren in the house too. 'You must meow loudly and point your face in the direction you want them to look at,' he'd explained. I was never able to meow as well as him but after some practice I could make Mrs A understand when I wanted to be let out into the courtyard or allowed back in.

Mrs A had a special name for me. 'Baby Cat,' she would whisper when I was in her arms, her voice as warm as Mama's breath.

The first time she'd tried to pick me up I'd bitten her. I didn't know her then and had thought she was attacking me. But she didn't yell or get angry. She'd just put me down gently and gone away to wash the bite. I had felt so ashamed.

I still hadn't wholly got used to the idea of Ren holding me but I didn't really think of Mrs A as a Ren anymore. She was kind of like a Ren-cat. Auntie Li on the other paw, was definitely not cat-like. Every chance she got she came and waved her broom at me, specially if I was up in the pomegranate tree.

I liked the tree very much. When I climbed it I could see into the sky and imagine the whole big World without having to leave the siheyuan. And when the pigeons flew across I thought that maybe they would carry some news of me to Mama and my brothers.

I knew that was a silly idea, which is why I never told Soyabean. But I couldn't help thinking it anyway. Thoughts could be like that sometimes. They just entered your head and stayed no matter how much you tried to tell them they were silly and should go away.

Soyabean said I had too many thoughts. Maybe he was right but perhaps he had too few? Certainly, at the moment he only seemed to have one big thought—to do with this modelling offer. I wasn't happy with the situation but he was so excited that I couldn't bring myself to say anything. Soyabean may have been big and brave but he was very emotional and got upset easily.

I'd been suspicious from the moment that Xiao Xu came around to make the offer.

'My friend has a pet food company and Soyabean will be the perfect model for its TV commercial,' he'd grinned at Mr and Mrs A. 'They'll pay well for it and imagine how famous your maomi will become!'

Why did he all of a sudden care so much about Soyabean? And where was Nai Nai? Why had he come without her? I had so many questions. There was something wrong with Xiao Xu. He made my whiskers stand up. I tried to tell Mr A not to agree but he didn't understand. It was so frustrating. I wished I could make Ren understand me better.

Mrs A was smiling at Soyabean who was jumping up and down, so she didn't notice me either. I was ducking under the table that all the Ren were sitting around and wasn't that easy to spot in any case. But I didn't want to come out in the open with Xiao Xu around. Nothing good could come from that Ren.

Now it was too late and Soyabean was to become the model for 'Maomi Deluxe,' premium cat food. Xiao Xu had said that his friend had big plans to sell this food all over China.

'It used to be that we kept a cat to catch a mouse. Nowadays we must buy a mouse to feed a cat!' Xiao Xu had laughed. It was a high-pitched, ugly sound and my whiskers immediately began to rise.

'There are a lot of people like you two in China today with money to spare,' Xiao Xu had said. 'Pet food is one of our biggest growth industries. Your Soyabean will make us all rich!'

Mr and Mrs A had never given us any Maomi Deluxe to eat so I had no idea how good it was but Soyabean couldn't wait to try it. His big first day as a model was fixed for next week and he was prancing around like he was already world famous.

I thought he should be careful with how much he was eating, especially now that he was going to be on TV. He was getting quite podgy. But I didn't want to hurt his feelings, so I said nothing. Maybe, I should stop letting him eat all my food too. But I would have to eat it then and I'm not sure my tummy could fit it all in.

Today Mrs A brought down our carry bags from on top of the closet in the storage room. That always meant one thing: a trip to the vet. I scurried off to hide under the bed where Mrs A couldn't reach for me and found Soyabean already there. It was funny because Soyabean was usually so fearless but when it came to going to the vet he was even more scared than I was.

Mrs A dangled Soyabean's favourite salami to get him to come out from under the bed. Of course, it worked. But I held back and in the end Auntie Li had to come and help Mrs A lift up the bed to drag me out.

I always felt panicky at the thought of going to the vet but once I was actually inside the carry bag and on the way I tended to calm down. There was nothing to be gained from struggling. The vet won no matter how much I fought and I'd learnt it was best to squeeze my eyes shut and make my mind go blank. This made the whole ordeal pass quicker.

But Soyabean would cry and yowl the whole while. He was forever saying how much he wanted to explore the World. Yet, when we were in the car and he finally had a chance to look around outside, he'd just curl up in his bag and refuse even to peek out.

When we reached the vet's, Mrs A asked the doctor, Chen Daifu, to take a look at Soyabean first since he had to be in top shape for the modelling job. But Soyabean crawled deeper and deeper into the bag no matter how much the vet tried to pull him out.

In the end Chen Daifu decided to examine him inside the bag itself. After a few minutes of feeling Soyabean up and down the vet withdrew his hands from the bag and pointed to a chart that hung over his table with a picture of a sleek, smiling cat. The caption at the top of the chart read: 'Ideal cat'.

Mrs A looked relieved.

At this point Soyabean decided to emerge into the open. As he crawled out of the bag, Chen Daifu caught sight of him for the first time. The doctor's eyes widened with shock and his hand flew to point to another chart in the far corner of the room. This one showed a picture of a huge, red-eyed beast with the caption: 'Obese cat'.

Mrs A pursed her lips.

Soyabean was now on a diet and got to eat only a few handfuls of some flavourless dry pellets that Mrs A went to a special shop to buy. But I couldn't bear to see him so depressed and I ate even less than usual so he could have more of my regular food. I loved the way he purred in delight when I pawed it over to him.

This morning I woke up a little earlier than usual; the sky was still grey with night. It was the day Soyabean had been waiting for. Xiao Xu was going to come around later to take him to the set of the commercial. For the moment though he was fast asleep on Mr and Mrs A's bed.

I preferred to spend the nights out in the courtyard where it was cooler and I could catch glimpses of the moon like I used to from the garbage can. I had a good, long stretch and then went up to the tree for a scratch. A tingly feeling crawled from the tips of my nails all the way up my body. Scratching was the loveliest thing and having a pomegranate tree to scratch on whenever I wanted was part of the good yunqi Madam Wang had said I had.

I realized it was really very early because even the birds were still asleep. It was peaceful sitting out there in the courtyard and I closed my eyes to better appreciate the breeze that rustled through my fur.

Suddenly a clattering sound shattered the silence. Something was up on the roof. I swung around at

once to look up, my claws extended and back arched. I knew I was only a small cat and scared of many things but I was quick and my teeth were sharp. The siheyuan was my home and no matter how frightened I was, I would do whatever it took to protect it.

But the sky was empty as it stretched beyond the grey tiles of the roof. I crouched down low on my haunches ready to spring up at any time and slowly turned around the yard, scanning the rooftop.

I froze.

A bony figure was slinking out from the shadows above the kitchen. It came to a halt and stared down at me. My heart beat galloped. It was a cat and a wild-looking one at that, with matted fur and hollow cheeks. I was so stunned that I forgot to make my fierce face. But just as I was about to collect myself, the intruder spoke.

'Number Three? Number three, is that you?' the cat croaked.

I felt dizzy, confused. Could it really be? Or was I dreaming like I had so many times in the past?

'Number three, it's me, your Da Ger,' said the cat, his voice stronger this time.

My eyes were thick with tears as I looked at the skinny animal, searching for some clue to confirm that this really was my big brother. His fur was so dirty the colour was unclear and he spoke with a funny accent adding an 'er' to the end of his sentences.

But there was something: maybe the way he held

his head, slouched forward. This really was Number One, my Da Ge.

'You look well, little Number Three,' smiled Da Ge and I saw he had several missing teeth.

I felt numb and hurt at the same time. Here I was eating egg yolk and fish every day and there was my brother, broken and starving. Why was our yunqi so different? Why had I been taken away from the dustbin while the rest of my family still roamed the streets? I found myself unable to say anything, filled with guilt at my round belly and tick-free skin.

'What's wrong, Number Three?' asked Da Ge, frowning. 'Aren't you happy to see me? I've been watching you for many days but I wasn't sure you'd want to meet me, so I stayed away. You have such a fine life now. Perhaps I shouldn't have come.'

'Of course I want to see you,' I burst out, squeaky with indignation. 'There is nothing I have ever wanted more! How are you, Da Ge? How did you find me? How is Mama? And the other brothers? Where have you been?'

Now that I had found my voice, I couldn't stop babbling.

'Hey kid! Slow down, slow down,' Da Ge laughed. 'Slow down and I'll tell you everything.' I sat back on my haunches waiting for him to begin. He looked at me a little sadly.

'Oh Number Three, I remember how much you used to love Mama's stories. I suppose we all did.' Da

Ge sighed but a second later was smiling widely again. The gaps between his teeth looked even bigger than before.

'After you left with the waiguo Ren, things changed for all of us. Mama got more and more moody and after a while she stopped coming home every evening. Some days we were so hungry that we'd lick the sides of the garbage can for any trace of thrown away food. But there was nothing.'

'It was terrible, Number Three. And even Old Man Zhao disappeared. We would wait for hours on the front lawn every morning for him to come out to exercise, but he didn't. Then one day a big van with a flashing light on top pulled up in front of the house and a group of Ren hurriedly carried the Old Man out on a stretcher. He was lying very still and we thought that maybe he was asleep.'

'But just before they put him inside the van I noticed him trying to raise his head towards the bushes where we were hiding. I think maybe he was hoping to see us. But we were so frightened with all the noise and Ren that we stayed put. They drove away and we never saw Old Man Zhao again.'

'We didn't really have a choice after that Number Three. We began to leave the dustbin and wander further and further to hunt for our own food. It was tough because we were still only kittens.'

'Madam Wang returned a few times with different Ren but they always looked disappointed when they saw us and shook their heads at her. We had too many fleas you see, and I guess we just weren't pretty enough to be pets. You were lucky to have been taken when Mama was still around to feed us properly.'

I felt the guilty pain in my stomach again, but Da Ge didn't pause in his story.

'Eventually, I left the campus. I no longer saw our brothers regularly and there was little point in staying. So, one morning I started to walk away and just kept walking. It was very hot and I was hungry, but I didn't feel too bad which was surprising considering my prospects.'

I was just about to ask Da Ge what 'prospects' meant when I remembered how much he used to enjoy using big words that I didn't understand, just to impress me. So I kept quiet. But the guilty knot in my tummy loosened and I almost felt like laughing. After so many months away from him it was taking only a few minutes to feel like we had never been apart.

'It was good to be out in the World,' my brother continued. 'You would probably have been scared Number Three, but I was excited.'

'There were many interesting things to look at and smell: Buildings so high you couldn't see where they ended; juicy lamb chuan'r on sticks being roasted over coals on street corners; shiny, yellow goldfish staring out of bowls stacked in the windows of shops.'

'And of course I'll never forget the first time I spotted a rat. I was so excited my teeth started chattering. I was too weak to run it down, but that didn't matter. There were just so many possibilities out there in the World,' my brother chuckled at the memory.

'I learnt quickly to keep away from the big roads. They were too loud and crowded with cars and buses always squealing and screeching. It wasn't safe for a cat to be out there. We might be quick but cars are quicker and they have no feelings because they are machines. It would only take a second for a cat to be crushed under their great wheels.' Da Ge shuddered.

'You be careful Number Three if you ever find yourself in the World among cars. They are not our friends. But of course you shouldn't worry if you are with your Ren. Cars obey Ren, you see.'

I had gone to the vet in a car many times, but I didn't say anything because I didn't want Da Ge to think I was showing off.

'After many days of walking, I finally found myself in the hutongs,' my brother picked up his story once again. 'I had remembered Mama telling us about the hutongs and their splendid siheyuan where our ancestor fatty Fei Fei lived. Of course many of the houses were now crumbling and old but I found that a cat could be happy there.'

'They were too narrow for cars and there was

always some food being cooked in the streets—stinky tofu or jian bing pancakes—that I could nick a bit of.'

'I was happy enough Number Three. But after a while it got a bit lonely. I had no friends; no one to share a juicy mouse with or lie down next to in the evening. It was difficult to admit it kid, but I missed Mama and our brothers.'

'Then one day I was walking past this temple. Do you know which one I'm talking about? It's only a few minutes from here with golden roofs and deep red walls. It's always crowded with Ren lighting these funny-smelling, smoky sticks. You don't? Well, I suppose you wouldn't, being stuck in here all day.'

'Anyway, it was in the early evening and I was walking past the temple on the way back to Chrysanthemum alley, where I was putting up for the time being, when I saw a large orange cat being savagely attacked by a group of 5 or 6 other cats. He was fighting back bravely but he was clearly in trouble, slowly being driven towards the wall of the temple, until he was backed up against it.'

'The whole scene got my blood boiling, Number Three, it did. One against so many was just not on now, was it? I suppose I knew it was probably best to mind my own business and move on, but before I could think too much, I found myself joining in the fight, scratching and biting the attackers for all I was worth.'

'Oh! It was glorious! With me to help, the orange

cat seemed to get a second wind and what a time we had biffing and hissing, mauling and tearing! We worked well as a team and it only took a few minutes before the cats were running away mewling like kitties with missing bits of ears and their tails between their legs.'

'I turned panting to face my new friend who despite the gashes on his face was smiling cheerfully. He quickly rubbed his nose against mine. "Whew! That was a close one, Ge Menr," he said. "Those tom cats from the Big Stone Alley Gang are getting a little too cocky these days." He paused to spit out a bloody tooth. "But we showed them, eh?"

'I was absolutely impressed Number Three. This was the coolest cat I had ever met and he'd called me "Ge Menr!" No one had ever called me their "mate" before. I felt I was floating on air.'

'He asked me which gang I belonged to and when I mumbled in embarrassment that I was all alone, he beamed back at me. "Well then, you'd better join my boys on Ghost Street, hadn't you," he said trotting off jauntily and waving his tail for me to follow.'

'My whiskers stood up Number Three, because it was only now that I realized I'd just met none other than the boss of the legendary Ghost Street Gang. Ghost Street as I'm sure even you know is the most sought after real estate in all of Beijing for dustbin cats.'

For once I knew what my brother was talking

about. Ghost Street was right round the corner from our siheyuan and we drove past it on the way to see Chen Daifu. It was a very pretty street, lined on each side with rows of restaurants with sparkling red lanterns hung up in front of them.

'The restaurants on Ghost Street never close Number Three,' Da Ge explained 'and there's always a little hairy crab that manages to scuttle away from the back door of a kitchen. But they can never get past the Ghost Street Gang of cats, no chance!'

'There's nothing like Ghost Street in all of Beijing, where a dustbin cat can go to bed every night on a full stomach of the choicest scraps: carp fin and bullfrog brains; pig's snout and chicken wings. It's a pretty sweet deal!'

'But don't you believe it's all eating and sleeping for us boys, Number Three. There isn't another gang in China that wouldn't give up their tails to take over from us. So we've got to fight to protect our space.'

'That Big Stone Bridge lot by the temple is the worst. I guess I can understand. It must be frustrating to live so close and yet so far from all that yummy Ghost Street food! Ha!' Da Ge laughed.

I had felt so sorry for my brother when I'd first seen him on the roof this morning but my heart felt lighter hearing that he was well and happy in his own way. I couldn't even have begun to imagine what life with a 'gang' would be like but I thought it wouldn't suit me. I didn't like fighting at all.

'Well, Number Three. That's pretty much my story. But you should know that through it all I thought of you often. You were always so sweet and worried about everything. It was a relief to know you were safe and loved. Life in the gangs wouldn't have been your bowl of milk.'

'But Da Ge, how did you find me?' I meowed curiously.

My brother's eyes twinkled. 'Little sister, you're in for a surprise.'

'Now, all us Ghost Street cats knew that the Boss had a son who lived in a nearby courtyard with a couple of waiguo Ren. You see whenever he went to pay his Tai Tai a visit on East Drum Tower Avenue she begged him to find out some news of the lad. So he made it a rule for someone or the other in the gang to swing by this waiguo Ren house to keep an eye on the kid; make sure he was doing okay.'

'Can you imagine my surprise when it was my turn to make the trip for the first time? It was in the evening, when the shadows are thick enough to hide in. I made it up right here on this end of the roof without being noticed and looked around for an orange young un', like I had been told to.'

'Instead, I saw you! You were so plump and pretty that I couldn't be totally sure it was you but then I spotted your mistress. I remembered her clearly from the time she'd come with Madam Wang to take you away. After all, who could forget someone with such a big nose? And I knew it was you down there!'

'I went running back to tell the Boss and he was tickled pink to know that his boy and my sis were shacking up together. And so now he's ordered the gang to look out for both of you.'

'We're all so proud of you two; how healthy and beautiful you are. As good as any pedigree. No one could imagine you were liulangmao.'

I winced.

'Liulangmao' was the term Ren used to refer to dustbin cats. It literally meant 'vagabond cat' but it was a bad, hurtful word. Mama used to get really furious if she ever heard anyone use it.

'Just because we live on the street doesn't mean we deserve less respect than the rarest pedigree,' she used to say, her ears stiff with anger.

'You should enjoy your life, Number Three,' Da Ge continued. 'And don't worry about me or the others. We know how to take care of ourselves. The boss is the coolest cat in town and none of us go hungry.'

'Actually I wouldn't have come to bother you at all, but we are a bit worried about the situation and thought that we should warn you two little ones to be careful.'

'What situation, Da Ge?' I said, frowning.

'Don't you know?' my brother asked back.

He looked around quickly before coming further down the roof, closer to me. Leaning forward he said in a low meow, 'Haven't you heard the news about the virus? Haven't you heard your master saying anything about it?'

A virus? I knew that was something that made you ill because Chen Daifu had said I had one when Mrs A had taken me to see him for the first time. He'd given me some bitter medicine to take that I always tried to spit out but I couldn't because Mrs A would close my snout until she was sure I'd swallowed it.

But I couldn't remember anything new about a virus. Or could I?

I thought hard and all at once I remembered the evening that Xiao Xu and Nai Nai had come over a few weeks ago. The As' friend, Mr J had mentioned something about a virus then that had made Xiao Xu very angry.

But I hadn't heard the conversation clearly because I'd been hiding in Mrs A's bedroom and only peeking out of the window every once in a while. What was it that Mr J had said? Wasn't it something about leaving Beijing because of a virus?

Mr and Mrs A hadn't seemed particularly worried and so I hadn't thought it very important. And Soyabean hadn't mentioned anything either. He was the one who spent more time around Ren picking up information. But of course his mind was totally full with dreams of modelling and becoming famous these days. So perhaps he hadn't been paying attention.

'Tell me everything Da Ge,' I said. 'We hardly leave the courtyard, so it's rare we get news of the World. What is going on with this virus? Are you safe?'

My brother sighed.

'I don't know, Number Three. Something very peculiar is happening. Ren are walking around with great white masks tied over their mouths so you can't see their lips when they talk. It's a frightening thing to see. Animals everywhere are worried. The birds are staying high up in the trees and refusing to fly down to the ground even to pick up crumbs. We don't see many dogs anymore. Their owners don't bring them out for walks like before. And we alley cats are worried too. There are so many rumours.'

He looked around quickly once again before going on.

'When things go wrong it's usually animals that Ren blame. Last year there was a virus they said came from chickens. It took just one Ren to die and they killed forty thousand chickens.'

'No, little Number Three, the World is not fair and when Ren get worried about a virus it usually means trouble for us animals.'

My tail felt heavy with dread and dropped down between my legs.

'What should we do Da Ge?' I asked.

My brother smiled and some of the gloom lifted from his face.

'You don't really need to worry Number Three,' he said. 'Your master and mistress are good Ren. They'll protect you, whatever happens. I'm sure of it. Just stay inside the siheyuan and keep away from . . .'

His voice trailed off as behind us the sound of a

curtain being drawn back was followed by that of a window opening. The Ren were up.

'I better go,' he said quickly and before I knew it he was bounding up and across onto the neighbour's roof.

'Xiao xin, Da Ge' I whispered as he disappeared into the bright morning sun, 'tread with a small heart, big brother.'

But of course, he couldn't hear me.

chapter five

SOYABEAN

Chinese Food for Chinese Cat

It was the fifth day of filming and I was expecting Xiao Xu to pick me up at any moment. I'd been ready for ages already. I did wish he'd hurry up. Mrs A had shampooed me last night and I smelt great. My fur felt super soft too. I was terribly hungry though. I couldn't wait to reach the set and bury my mouth in a full bowl of yummy Maomi Deluxe.

This diet business was simply awful and also so unnecessary. Chen Daifu must have been out of his mind.

Obese cat? Me?

Nonsense! I was gorgeous. Everyone said so.

I was a model. I sincerely doubted Chen Daifu could ever be a model. But of course, Mrs A listened to everything that doctor told her and she'd been feeding me water and teaspoons of food ever since.

If it hadn't been for Tofu's meals, which I was usually able to sneak most of, I wouldn't have had the energy to get around at all. Thankfully, Xiao Xu tended to bring a few snacks along with him which kept me going in the car. It was quite a long drive out to the set, almost outside the city.

Although I didn't have much time to look out of the window being busy wolfing down Xiao Xu's treats, it was an interesting drive. So many very tall buildings, rising up higher than even birds could fly. Sometimes I wished we lived in one of these fancy, modern apartments instead of in the hutong, where it was always dirty and a little smelly. Not quite the appropriate address for a model.

Xiao Xu said that when we were all rich thanks to my Maomi Deluxe ad, he'd leave the Xu courtyard and move into one of the new high-rise buildings. He'd already got some projects lined up in the real-estate business. I knew from the way that he said it that this must be a good thing. Xiao Xu's life was so exciting. Not boring like Mr and Mrs A's.

To think, I didn't like him earlier. I couldn't really think why. It was all because of him that I was a model now and he was always very nice to me. He brought me snacks, behind Mrs A's back, and had a special velvet pillow in his car for me to rest on. 'You're a lovely, plump goldmine, you are, Soyabean,' he would say rubbing my head.

Life was good. But it would have been even better if only Tofu would cheer up. She'd become such a pain. Always going on and on about how I should be careful of Xiao Xu.

I'd explained to her that we had been wrong about him, but she didn't believe me. To be honest, I thought she was a little jealous. It was natural. I would soon be on TV and everyone admired me so much. But no one ever noticed her. How could they? She was always lurking around in corners.

Well, I forgave her. It couldn't have been easy living with a star.

Liu Libo said it should be a wrap today since we had already been filming for five days. 'A wrap' means 'finished' in the advertising world. I explained this to Tofu but she didn't seem very interested.

Liu Libo was the big boss which is why everyone simply called him Liu Laoban, Liu the boss. He owned the company that made Maomi Deluxe. But Xiao Xu said this was only one of his various businesses. At first I hadn't liked him much because he had black teeth and his mouth smelled. But he'd been very supportive during the filming.

He made sure I got extra Maomi Deluxe at the end of the day, which was just as well because Mrs A had nothing waiting for me at home. And after watching me perform a take or two of the ad, he always laughed loudly and slapped Xiao Xu on the back.

'That's a class-A maomi you've found me ge menr,' he'd say.

What I'd learnt from all this was that a cat shouldn't be so hasty to judge. I'd been telling Tofu: 'first impressions can be wrong'. Predictably she ignored me. I guess she really was very jealous, poor thing.

The one thing that puzzled me was why Nai Nai never came along with Xiao Xu for the filming. I was disappointed the first time he came to get me without her. I'd been looking forward to her scratching my belly in the heavenly way only she could.

But then I got so busy on the set that I didn't have time to miss her. Perhaps it was just as well she didn't come. She was a bit old after all and might not have fit in on the set.

It got very busy when we began filming. Liu Laoban gave all the orders and there were at least a dozen Ren scurrying around the place with cameras and lights. The ad was less than a minute long but we had to shoot it again and again. I played my role perfectly, but the Ren actors often made a mistake.

This was how it went: The scene began with me sitting in what was supposed to be the kitchen of one of those modern new apartments when one of the actors, a man called Lu, walked in.

'Time for dinner maomi,' he said and put down a bowl filled with food taken out of a packet with waiguo writing all over it. This was to let viewers know that the packet contained some fancy, waiguo food.

But instead of eating the dinner, I had to lie around

looking sick, refusing to go to the bowl even though the man was encouraging me to. That part was really difficult because I was usually starving by this time.

Then finally the man's Tai Tai, an actress called Zhao, entered. She took in the scene and shook her head.

'Old Lu,' she said to her husband. 'When you come home in the evening would you rather have a steaming plate of fried pork noodles or a cold, crusty sandwich?'

'Noodles,' replied Lu at once.

'Of course you would, because Chinese food is better,' said Ms Zhao, her hands on her hips. 'But then why should maomi be any different?'

At this point she walked over to a shelf and took down a box of Maomi Deluxe, the Chinese characters on the packet flashing clearly. She threw away the food Lu had poured out for me and replaced it with Maomi Deluxe.

This was my favourite part of the ad because I now had to jump up from the floor and go bounding to the bowl in excitement and begin to eat the food enthusiastically. I had to confess I hardly needed to act the scene out. It came very naturally to me.

Once I began eating, Ms Zhao turned to the camera holding the box of Maomi Deluxe in her hand and said, 'Chinese food for Chinese cat because after all Chinese food is better!'

All the Ren on the set complimented my acting and

said how realistic it was which made me happy, but I did sometimes feel a twinge of guilt. I wasn't sure I liked the way the ad put down waiguo cat food. Mr and Mrs A were waiguo Ren after all.

In fact, before I had been put on that unnecessary diet, Mrs A had often given me waiguo cat food out of a packet very much like the one that Lu fed me from at the beginning of the ad. And it was really tasty. Actually, funnily enough it was quite similar to Maomi Deluxe.

But I'd realized it was best to put all these thoughts out of my head and focus on the job at paw; the big picture was more important than details. It wasn't easy, though. There were so many distractions when one was famous. Everyone in our hutong knew that I was going to be on TV soon and neighbours were constantly knocking on the siheyuan doors, asking to come in and take a look at me.

Yesterday, Xiao Wang from the house next door came by with a cricket as a present for me. The insect was caged inside a box but I caught glimpses of it through the bamboo weave. It was bright green and chirping in the most exciting way. I patted the box around and was getting ready to claw the cricket out when to my horror Mrs A tried to return the present to Xiao Wang.

'Xie Xie,' she thanked the boy. 'But Xiao Wang we couldn't possibly accept your cricket.'

I could tell by her tone that she didn't really want

the insect at all. 'But it's for me!' I wanted to tell her. Mrs A was strangely frightened of bugs. She would scream if she saw a spider. Ren could be odd.

'Tai Tai, this is a present for your maomi,' insisted Xiao Wang. 'We're all so excited to have a TV star living right next door. Maybe the government will start paying us some attention now that a celebrity lives here. My Ma has been hoping that they might put in a flush in the hutong toilet. We've heard that some of the nearby hutongs have had their toilets upgraded. It would really improve the smell around here if we got a flush too.'

'You know what it's like, Tai Tai. The government only spends money on places where important people live. No one important has ever lived here. But now your maomi will be on TV advertising some big company's pet food. Perhaps things will finally change around here.'

Mrs A had looked embarrassed. 'Well then, thank you very much for your present Xiao Wang,' she'd said, much to my relief. 'I'm sure Soyabean appreciates it.'

Then after a pause she'd added. 'Would you like to go to the toilet by any chance?'

Xiao Wang's eyes had shone bright with excitement. 'Could I really, Tai Tai?'

Mrs A had then nodded quickly and showed him the way.

You see, most Ren who lived in the hutongs were

quite poor and most siheyuan didn't have private toilets. But the As' courtyard was a special, expensive, waiguo Ren one, with a private toilet and flush; a big deal for Ren.

I'd overheard Auntie Li describing it to the hutong neighbours when she went out to the xiao mai bu, the corner shop, outside. The shop was right opposite the kitchen and if I jumped up to the window sill set high on the wall, I could look out onto the street and hear what was going on.

'There are dark-blue tiles on the floor,' she'd told a group of open-mouthed neighbours. 'There is a sink with two taps, one for hot and the other for cold water.'

'Can they get hot water in the mornings as well as the evenings?' Old Lady Fang, the xiao mai bu owner had asked.

'They can get hot water 24 hours of the day,' replied Auntie Li drawing unbelieving gasps from her audience.

I must say I felt quite sorry for Ren. Their lives were so complicated. Cats could make a toilet anywhere, but Ren needed pipes and flushes and taps. Xiao Xu said that one of the reasons he was so keen to move into the new, high-rise buildings was that every apartment had its own toilet. Toilets played a big role in Ren's lives.

After Xiao Wang had left, Mrs A picked up the bamboo box with the cricket. I'd scampered behind her expecting her to hand it over to me, since this was my present, but instead she'd gone to a window and let the cricket out of the box and into the hutong.

I was quite annoyed to see it scuttle away. It was unfair how Mrs A had let my present go just like that.

I'd gone off in a sulk, looking for Tofu but of course she was nowhere to be seen.

I don't know how that cat managed to disappear so much, so often. I hadn't seen her all morning today either. Not that she was much fun to be around these days. I couldn't bear the way she'd taken to looking at me all gloomy and reproachful.

There was a loud rapping on the door. I assumed it was Xiao Xu. He'd certainly taken his time getting there this morning. I went bounding up to the door and meowed loudly for a Ren to come and open up. Mrs A stepped out of the main pavilion, her hair still wet from her morning bath, and walked slowly across the yard.

'Hurry up,' I meowed.

'Patience Soyabean,' she replied, 'I'm coming.'

It was wonderful how well we could communicate.

She reached the front doors and threw them open only to take a big step backwards looking startled. It wasn't Xiao Xu after all but Fat Tao from down the lane. He was wearing his usual torn, sleeveless vest but a dirty white mask was stretched across his face, so you could only see his beady eyes. Usually, he glanced downwards whenever Mr or Mrs A walked by. Many of the hutong Ren were like that. I supposed they were not quite sure how to talk to waiguo Ren.

But today, he looked at Mrs A aggressively. He held up a large piece of paper with some kind of a picture on it. I'd been hiding behind Mrs A's legs, a little scared by his strange appearance, but I poked my head out from between them to get a better look.

It was the most awful picture, of a Ren sitting down to a meal with a bowl in from of him and chopsticks in his hand. But the part that made my tummy go cold is what was in the Ren's bowl. It was unmistakably a cat. Was the Ren going to eat the cat? Was that possible? My heart started to beat very, very fast. There was a big, red slash that ran across the picture, right through the middle of the cat.

What did it mean?

I shrank back behind the safety of Mrs A's legs.

'What is it Fat Tao,' she asked in an unusually sharp tone. 'What is all this?'

'Where are those two maomi of yours?' drawled Fat Tao. His voice was muffled from behind the mask.

'And what business is that of yours?' replied Mrs A. 'What is this poster you are carrying?'

'You better keep an eye on those maomi Tai Tai,' continued Fat Tao, quite rudely.

I could see long hairs escaping the arch of his eyebrows. I didn't like the way he smelt at all. Like old meat.

'Don't you know that it is cats that are giving everyone that terrible virus, bing du?' he continued.

'Look,' he held up his poster. 'The government has put these up everywhere. It's telling us not to eat any cats because they carry bing du with them, the dirty animals.'

'Fat Tao,' said Mrs A, more calmly now. 'No one here is planning to eat any cat. You can be rest assured. And as for bing du and cats, you have no idea what you are talking about. There is some evidence that the virus might be linked to *civet* cats, but those are as different from Tofu and Soyabean as a tiger. So, if you wouldn't mind, I'm very busy this morning.'

Fat Tao slowly peeled off his mask and spat right outside the courtyard door. It made an ugly, splashing sound.

'I'll be going then, but you better keep your two maomi inside your house if you know what's good for you. And get some masks for yourself. In fact, get some for those blasted cats too. We don't want them walking around our hutong infecting us poor folk with bing du, celebrity cat or not. You rich waiguo ren may be able to afford the hospital fees but we can't afford to take any chances at all.'

Mrs A closed the doors on Fat Tao. Her face was pale and she was shaking. She rushed across to Mr A's study. It was early and he still hadn't left for work. I ran behind her.

'That was that lout Fat Tao,' said Mrs A going into the study without knocking.

Mr A looked up from his desk. 'Well, what did he want?'

'I'm worried love,' she answered. 'He was making some kind of threat about the cats. Claiming that they cause bing du and we should be careful. He had this awful poster with him warning people not to eat cats. As if we would! Do you think J was right? Is it no longer safe in Beijing? Should we leave? It's getting unbearable, with everyone wandering around the city with masks on, like a bunch of crazy surgeons.'

'Calm down darling,' Mr A stood up and put his arm around his wife.

'We've already talked about this. I think all the bing du talk is overblown hype. The real problem is down south in Hong Kong and Guangzhou. We're really quite safe up here in Beijing.'

'There've only been a dozen or so cases reported here and this is a city of 17 million people! Far greater chance of someone dying just crossing the road or from the vile air we have to breathe here than from this virus.'

He took a slow breath before continuing.

'And what would happen to the cats if we left? We couldn't take them with us at such short notice now, could we?'

Mrs A buried her head in his chest.

'I guess not,' she said. Her voice was muffled.

They left the study together and went into the living room but I stayed behind. I was so confused.

Tofu had been going on about some virus as well. She kept muttering something about her Da Ge landing up at the courtyard to warn us. I wished I'd paid more attention but I'd been so busy with the shooting and that stupid diet didn't leave me with much energy.

Where was she? And where was Xiao Xu? How come he hadn't said anything about this bing du virus? I was sure he would have if it really was all that serious. Xiao Xu always knew what was going on. He had many well-connected friends. Like Liu Laoban.

My heart beat began to slow down.

Perhaps all this talk was just Tofu and a few Ren getting all worked up about nothing. Liu Laoban hadn't mentioned anything. Even Mr A had just said there wasn't much to worry about in Beijing.

My tail began to rise and I trotted out into the yard feeling my usual confidence returning. I was a very brave cat after all. A virus didn't scare me. I just wished everyone would pay more attention to really important things like the Maomi Deluxe ad instead of acting all crazy about some silly bing du.

'Now do you believe me?' asked Tofu softly, suddenly appearing in front of me.

Her eyes were large and round as always.

'You startled me,' I said crossly. 'And where have

you been anyway? I've been looking everywhere for you.'

'I've been around,' she replied vaguely, 'and I heard everything. It's just like Da Ge said. When things start to go wrong for Ren they blame animals for it. We've got to be very careful Soyabean, your Ba has sent a warning.'

I couldn't help snorting. Tofu also seemed to imagine that her Da Ge and my Ba were somehow part of some gang that lived nearby, sending us regular messages to be careful. She spent too much time mooning around up in the pomegranate tree, in my opinion.

I also thought she needed to eat more. Anyone would start imagining things on as little food as she ate. I immediately felt a little guilty because maybe she would eat more if I didn't polish off most of her food. But then I reminded myself that it wasn't my fault she didn't *want* to eat. She *volunteered* to give me her food.

'Soyabean,' said Tofu urgently, interrupting my thoughts, 'always be on your guard when you leave the courtyard with Xiao Xu. And be careful of him too. He's a huai dan, a bad egg, that one. Don't get too close.'

There she was going on again. But I was saved from having to reply by another loud knock.

'Where's my favourite maomi?' boomed a voice from behind the doors. Xiao Xu had finally arrived!

chapter six

TOFU

Hot Air in the Mouth

I felt I was losing Soyabean. He just didn't seem to hear me anymore. The closer he got to that creepy Xiao Xu, the further away from me he went. If only he'd listen to his brain instead of his stomach.

I was so worried about everything: Soyabean getting pulled into Xiao Xu's net and not having had any news from Da Ge since that one time he'd come by. And then there was all this talk about bing du, the virus.

Even Mr and Mrs A were getting concerned. I could see it in Mrs A's eyes. She didn't go out as much as before. And Auntie Li had started to come to the siheyuan wearing a mask over her mouth. Could a mask keep out bing du? I didn't like masks. They erased too much of the face.

Fat Tao hadn't been around again but nor had the other neighbours. Not even Xiao Wang. I couldn't help thinking they were keeping away because of Soyabean and me.

Hadn't Fat Tao said that the virus came from cats? Did they really believe this? My paws clenched thinking about it.

The wind blew through my fur. There was a sharpness to it I hadn't noticed before. The leaves had begun to fall off the pomegranate tree these last few days and it was getting dark earlier.

The Maomi Deluxe ad played for the first time on TV yesterday. Soyabean stared at the screen all day long. Every time the ad came on he meowed loudly.

That cat! Hadn't his Mama told him that it was the tall flowers that get cut down first? And what was all that nonsense about 'Chinese food is better'?

I wasn't a very smart cat and there were many things I didn't know but I did know that there was something wrong in making a statement like that. Maybe some Ren liked Chinese food more and some preferred waiguo food but how could you say that Chinese food was always better? Even though I wasn't so interested in food at all, I still thought it was more interesting to have many different kinds of foods than just one type all the time.

It was almost evening now and there was no sign of Da Ge. I'd been scanning the roof for hours. Sometimes I thought I saw a movement and my heart leapt into my mouth in hope, but it was only a passing cloud. I hoped very much that my brother was well. A big lump swelled in my throat when I imagined what might happen if someone like Fat Tao caught hold of him.

The clouds were gathering fast now. I could smell rain in the wind. Soyabean was inside the living room glued to the TV set again. I supposed I should go join him. I could barely hear myself outside, the wind was groaning so.

I pushed open the cat flap the As had built into the main pavilion door and went through. It was much warmer inside. Mrs A was sitting on the sofa reading a newspaper. I went up close and leapt into her lap.

'Hello, Baby Cat,' she said and tickled me under the chin. I felt happiness jump up in my tummy. You're a pretty little owl you are, she murmured.

Of course she didn't really think I was an owl. It was just her way of telling me she loved me. I snuggled deeper into her arms. I hoped she knew I loved her too.

I heard purring and looked up to see that Soyabean had finally left his spot in front of the TV and had come to join us. The three of us cuddled up together in a jumble of hands and paws. Soyabean's belly was soft and comfortable against my ears. It had been ages since we had spent time like this together.

Maybe everything would be alright after all, I thought. This bing du virus couldn't last forever and now that the Maomi Deluxe ad had been made perhaps Xiao Xu would lose interest in Soyabean. Things could go back to how they used to be.

Just as I was being lulled into a soothing snooze a loud thunderclap brought Mrs A to her feet. 'Gosh! That was loud,' she said brushing us aside.

She hurried outside to shut the kitchen windows which were banging in the wind. I didn't want her to be alone and so I followed her out even though I was quite frightened by all the noise. We'd only just stepped out when the rain started coming down. I could barely see; the water was like a thick curtain.

Mrs A had opened an umbrella but it kept blowing away. She struggled to hold on to it with one hand while dragging the garden furniture under an awning with the other. Mr A was still at work and Auntie Li had left for the day. I was annoyed that Soyabean had stayed inside although I suppose he couldn't really have helped. But he could have shown some moral support.

Mrs A finally managed to get the furniture out of the rain and called out to me. I struggled against the wind to make my way over to her and had almost reached when a flash of lightening set the sky above the siheyuan ablaze in yellow-white light. The hair on my neck crackled.

Something was up there on the roof. I was sure it was Da Ge. What was he doing out here in weather like this?

Everything turned dark again, the heavy rain making it more difficult then ever to see clearly. 'Da Ge! Da Ge! Is that you?' I called out as loudly as I could, but my voice was carried away by the wind.

I could hear Mrs A shouting for me but I had to find out if Da Ge was really up there. I found myself by the pomegranate tree and decided to try and climb it to get closer to the roof. The trunk was slippery and the branches were swaying wildly. I made it half-way up before loosing my balance and crashing to the bottom.

'Tofu, come away from there at once,' yelled Mrs A, marching angrily towards me.

I needed to get away from her and to find my brother. He could be in trouble. But there was nowhere to hide. I was feeling desperate. Hot tears filled my eyes mingling with the cold rain.

'Kai Menr! Open the door, open up at once,' a sharp voice cut through the wind, followed by a rat-a-tat-tat hammering on the front door.

'Oh great! That's all I need: visitors!' Mrs A snapped as she turned away from me, towards the entrance.

'I'm coming, stop breaking the door down. It had better not be you again Fat Tao.'

'Open up quickly. It's the police,' came the reply.

'The police?' Mrs A quickened her step.

'What can I do for you at this time of the day, sir,' she asked pulling open the gates. She was soaking wet by now. A frog-faced policeman in uniform stood on the other end sheltering under a large umbrella.

'It has come to our attention that two waiguo ren are living in this hutong. As per the Chinese law on aliens, they must register with the local police station within 24 hours. At this point in time they are in contravention of the law of the People's Republic of China. They should be very sorry for their mistake.'

'Sir, is there any particular reason you keep referring to me in the third person plural?' Mrs A spat back.

The policeman spluttered, 'What do you mean?'

'I mean I am very obviously one of those waiguo ren you are talking about. In any case sir, I have already registered with the police more than a year ago, as has my husband. What is the problem all of a sudden? Why have you come here in this rain?'

'Madam, the rain is no obstacle for the Chinese police. No weather can stop us from carrying out our duties. You say, you have registered more than a year ago. But don't you know that you must renew this registration every year? By allowing your registration to lapse you have broken the laws of the People's Republic of China.'

'Oh? Well then, we'll come down first thing tomorrow morning to renew our registration, officer,' said Mrs A, rain streaming down her face. 'There's really nothing I can do about this now. It's pouring rain.'

The policeman held up his palm to silence her. He

was a very short Ren and barely reached Mrs A's shoulder.

'Madam, please not the rain again. You must apologize to the People's government immediately. Write a self-criticism detailing your lapse and promising never to make the same mistake again.'

'Are you serious?' asked Mrs A shaking her head.

'Of course I am serious. You waiguo ren should learn to be more serious. With the bing du virus going around it is of vital importance that we have all your details so that we can inform you in a timely manner of all developments relevant to your own safety in the event of any problem.'

The policeman paused for a second before hastily adding. 'Not that there is any problem. There is nothing to panic about at all. So it's very important that you remember: under no circumstances must you panic.'

Mrs A looked confused.

'I'm not panicking officer, don't worry.' Her eyes narrowed with suspicion. 'Unless there is something to panic about?'

'Absolutely not!' shouted the policeman. 'There is nothing to panic about. You must remember: do not panic!'

'Look, we're not getting anywhere,' said Mrs A impatiently. 'It's cold and windy and why don't you come inside and we can discuss it further? My husband should be home any moment and maybe we can just renew the registration now, okay?'

After a moment's hesitation the policeman agreed.

'Very well then,' he said, 'let's go in.' He tried to step across the entrance but his umbrella got caught in the doorway. It was too large to fit through.

As he struggled to close it I saw Da Ge pad across the boundary wall of the siheyuan opposite ours. My brother! It was him. I was sure of it.

In a second I was through the doors running after him. But even before I could reach the wall Da Ge disappeared, eaten up by the rain. I looked left and then right. He was gone.

I felt exhausted. My paws were hurting from cuts they'd got when I had slipped off the pomegranate tree and I was very cold by now. I was so disappointed with myself. What a useless cat I was. There was no point in trying to go after Da Ge now. It was too dark and rainy to see anything clearly. It was best to go home.

I turned around to make my way back and in that moment knew that I had just made the worst mistake of my life. The blood red gates of the As' siheyuan were firmly closed, locking me out in the hutong. Not even a chink of light escaped through them. A creeping dread inched over me. I had never been out in the World on my own before.

I scratched frantically at the door and tried to meow as loudly as I could but I knew even as I tried that no one inside would be able to hear me. How long would it be before Mrs A noticed I was missing? It could be ages.

But what about Soyabean? I felt a flashing hope. Soyabean would notice I wasn't around, wouldn't he? And he was so good at talking with Ren. He'd be able to bring it to Mrs A's notice and she would come running out to look for me and I would be right here outside the door waiting. Then we'd all go inside and she would dry me with a large, soft towel and kiss me and call me Baby Cat.

I knew I just had to sit tight and try to stay calm. But that was easier to think than do. Everything felt so unfamiliar out there. The big tree just outside our siheyuan seemed to have come alive. Its leaves shifted restlessly in the wind and its branches hung low like unsheathed claws.

I'd never seen the hutong like this. Usually it was bustling with life: Xiao Wang sitting under the tree playing with his crickets while other neighbours huddled outside Old Lady Fang's shop on low stools playing cards and cracking sunflower seeds. Old Lady Fang's yappy little dog Eraser was often out with them begging for bits to eat.

I couldn't believe I was even missing Eraser. I didn't like dogs much.

But in the rainy night the World was deserted. And yet I could sense things moving out of sight, on the margins. All manner of creatures could have been out here in the corners, prowling on rooftops, sniffing in dustbins. Not just dogs but even huang shu lang, the yellow weasels that slunk around gobbling up chickens and sparrows. I was only a very small cat. I didn't think I'd be safe if a huang shu lang came by.

I shivered with fright and cold. It was difficult to tell how much time had passed. It felt like a very, very long time. I knew I had to be patient. It couldn't be long now before the policeman would leave and those doors would open with Mrs A on the other side.

The rain had begun to soften into a drizzle and the wind was dying down. My ears pricked up. I could hear the hum of a car in the distance. There were very few cars in the hutongs. Most Ren who lived here rode bicycles, but the As had a car. It occurred to me that perhaps it was Mr A coming back from work. As the sound became louder I grew terribly excited at the thought of rescue. I had been bad but I'd learnt my lesson. I promised myself I would never leave the courtyard again.

But as the car loomed closer I saw it wasn't the As' blue car at all but a large, white van. There was something horribly frightening about that van. I could smell the danger coming from it. I knew I should try and hide but it was coming towards me so fast, its huge, bright headlights pinning me to the spot.

I tried to scrunch up by the door hoping that the van would drive past but instead it came to a screeching halt just before me. The driver's door opened creakily.

'Run Number Three, run!'

I looked around wildly. Da Ge was standing on our siheyuan's roof, meowing so desperately it sounded like a cry.

'Run kid!' he howled and I finally found my feet.

But just as I was about to bolt a rough hand yanked me up by the scruff of my neck.

'Got you!' chuckled the Ren who had come out of the van. He had long, jagged fingernails that dug into my skin. I yelped in pain.

'That should teach you, you vermin carrying filth,' he sneered holding me up in front of him.

He carried me around to the back of the van and although I tried to bite and hiss as much as I could his grip remained firm.

'Jump out of that van Number Three. Find a way to jump out of that van,' Da Ge cried out in the distance. 'We'll come and find you. Don't worry about anything. The Ghost Street gang will find you. Just get out somehow.'

I struggled to raise my head and answer my brother but the way the Ren was holding me was suffocating. I couldn't move my head. He finally relaxed his grip for a second as he opened the van's back door and I immediately sank my teeth into his fat finger.

'Ouch,' he yelled. I felt a brief moment of satisfaction before a stinging blow on the side of my head made everything go black inside me. The door to the back of the van slammed shut. I felt myself falling.

'Tofu, are you alright?'

My eyes flew open. Who else was in there? Who had spoken? I couldn't believe what I was seeing. A dozen or more dogs and cats of every size were squeezed in together in that small space. And looming up above me was none other than Eraser, Old Lady Fang's yappy dog.

'Are you hurt?' Eraser asked again, looking concerned.

'And why should you care what happens to this melon of a cat?' a long-nosed dog asked from a corner. 'You're a dog. Try to remember that instead of acting like some cross-eyed cat-lover. It's all because of these darned cats that we dogs are in this mess to begin with.'

'That's right,' barked a curly-haired poodle. 'It's these cats that are giving everyone the bing du virus. So why should dogs have to pay for it? It's not fair is it? I think we should give these feline friends of ours a lesson they won't forget,' he snarled bearing his long, yellow teeth.

'Silence!' a deep voice boomed and immediately a hush descended on the dogs.

'You fools,' spat out a large, brown dog from the back. I could tell from the lines on his face that he was old but his voice was steady. His body was covered in scars and a deep gash ran across his snout giving him a frightening look.

He was the kind of large dog that Ren called cai gou, food dog. Unlike the small, snapping Pekinese and Pomeranians that Ren liked to keep as pets, cai guo were meant for a different purpose. They were food. To be eaten in soup in the winter.

'Don't you realize that we're all being taken to our death? And all you fools can do is try to gang up on a bunch of helpless cats? What's the big difference between dogs and cats anyway? We're all animals and at the end of the day we're all the same to Ren: dispensable. This time it's the cats they say carry the virus. But that doesn't stop them rounding us dogs up does it?'

'And when they go around killing dogs for spreading rabies, no matter if the dogs are healthy, it doesn't stop them from getting rid of a cat or two at the same time. Here you are trying to blame everything on the cats. But you're just playing the same dirty game as Ren. I shouldn't even bother trying to bark some sense into your thick heads. In a little while you'll all just be dead meat in any case. As dead as a cai gou's future!' he said, lifting his head and laughing.

No one else joined in the laughter but the other dogs weren't looking at me in a threatening way any more.

Eraser put his wet nose to mine.

'We're lao pengyou, old friends, aren't we Tofu?' he asked.

I nodded weakly unable to focus. The image of Da Ge shouting out to me to jump out of the van filled my mind. But I was trapped. The door was tightly shut and the van was speeding away.

'Where are we going Eraser?' I found my voice with some difficulty.

I would have to be brave I told myself. Da Ge would come find me soon. I just had to find some way of escaping.

'Who knows Tofu?' the dog replied. 'The cai gou over there told us that gangs of Ren have been rounding up all the cats and dogs they find on the street and taking them away to a place from where they never come back. They choose rainy nights in particular because our owners are indoors and don't notice immediately when we get taken.'

'It's because of the bing du virus that's been going around. They blame us animals for it, especially cats. Oh, I'm so scared, Tofu! I miss Old Lady Fang and I know she'll be awfully worried about me. And it's really not good for her to worry. Whenever the Daifu comes around he always tells her not to worry. She has a weak heart you see. And now she'll be worrying and upsetting her heart, all because of me.'

Eraser sniffed loudly before going on.

'Ai! How I wish I had never gone out on a night like this. But I really had to go relieve myself. I'd already been holding it in for hours and hours. Or at least it felt like hours and hours. And I'm a big dog now, fully toilet trained. It just wouldn't have done for me to make a mess inside the house, would it? Old Lady Fang wouldn't have liked it at all.'

'How was I to know that this would happen? I was only outside for a few minutes and hadn't even finished my business properly when this van pulled up next to me and a Ren got out and shoved me in here.'

Eraser sniffed again, tears beginning to stream down his face. 'I'm so afraid Tofu. I haven't ever been away from Old Lady Fang since I was four weeks old.'

'Don't worry so much Eraser,' I found myself saying although I was terrified myself.

'We just have to find a way to get out of this van. If we do my Da Ge and his friends will come to help us and take us back home. Everything will be okay.'

Eraser looked at me with sad, wet, eyes and didn't reply. 'Everything will be okay,' I said again, but the words felt like hot air in my mouth.

chapter seven

SOYABEAN

Protein

I was sick with worry. My stomach heaved and I couldn't even get my breakfast down today. Tofu's empty bowl lay next to mine staring accusingly at me. Where was she? How was she? She'd simply vanished into the rain.

I was so ashamed of myself. How could I have not noticed that she'd disappeared? It was that dratted Maomi Deluxe ad.

I'd been too busy waiting for it to come on again, to pay attention to anything else. Mrs A had been busy with the policeman and in the end we'd only realized Tofu was gone after Mr A had returned home and asked where she was. It was already late at night by then and very dark. I felt terrible imagining Tofu out in the World, lost and all alone by herself.

Mr and Mrs A had immediately gone out to look for her with big torches, but I had had to stay back in the courtyard. They were gone for hours and I'd just sat there in the yard, the cold seeping into my skin. I'd realized then that I wasn't brave and I wasn't wonderful. I was only a stupid cat; a bad cat. A very bad cat who had let down his best friend.

When Mr and Mrs A finally returned, without Tofu, they'd gone straight to bed but I heard Mrs A sobbing through the night. I hadn't been able to sleep either.

Tofu had warned me that we needed to be careful so many times. How could I have ignored her? And when I should have been looking out for her I was too busy watching TV instead.

I knew in my whiskers that something was very wrong. Tofu was not the kind of cat to go off wandering by herself. Something dreadful must have happened. Could Fat Tao have got to her? I remembered that awful poster he had brought along the other day and shivered.

Auntie Li had gone to speak with the neighbours this morning to ask if anyone had seen Tofu last night. She wasn't back yet and we were all waiting for her in the kitchen. Mrs A was reading the newspaper, her eyes rimmed red. Mr A was pacing up and down the room.

'This miserable virus!' Mrs A suddenly exclaimed pushing her newspaper away. 'And you!' she continued glaring at Mr A. 'I can't believe you've been saying we have nothing to worry about all this time. Have you read the paper? The government has finally come out and admitted that it's not just a handful of people infected with bing du in Beijing but several hundred. And who knows if it's really only several hundred? Can we believe anything this government says?'

'J was right. We should have left this city ages ago. We could have found a way to take the cats with us if we'd tried. And now with the virus spreading so fast perhaps it's too late. What if they quarantine the city? What if we can't get out? And what will happen to my baby? Oh! my sweet Baby Cat. Where is she? What have they done to her?'

Mrs A broke down crying and Mr A put his arms around her without saying anything. I curled up in a little ball feeling my heart break into sharp, painful pieces.

'I just saw Fat Tao.' Auntie Li was back. She took off her jacket and folded it on a chair.

'Well?' Mr A asked.

'That Fat Tao is no good, I tell you,' she replied, walking over to the stove to boil some water for tea. 'These Beijing ren, they make fun of us migrant workers from the countryside. They think we're dirty and uncultured. 'Tu' they call us, 'dirt.' But 'tu' also means soil. It's from that soil that we grow the food that feeds city folk.'

'Yes, our accents might be different but I ask you

what's so cultured about looking down on folk just because they're poor?'

Auntie Li was from a far-away province in southern China. I'd heard her telling Mrs A that in her village Ren had to catch rats to eat, just like cats, because there was nothing else for them to cook. She often grumbled about the way city Ren looked down on her. Her stories used to make Tofu very sad. You see, Tofu was a dustbin cat herself.

'He didn't even ask me to take a seat,' Auntie Li continued as she poured freshly boiled water into a teapot. 'I asked him if he'd seen Tofu and he just sniggered. I can't stand how stinky his breath is. He might be a hot-shot city dweller, but he obviously doesn't brush his teeth.'

'But Auntie Li, what did he say about Tofu,' Mrs A asked, her voice sounding thin and weak.

'That he hadn't seen her but that she'd obviously got what she deserved. He reckoned Soyabean was lucky to have been spared but that you "waiguo ren" had better keep an eye on him too. He said he'd been around here to warn you two already and you should have paid more attention to him.'

'He's a wicked one, that Fat Tao, Mrs A,' Auntie Li took a long sip of her hot tea, 'a real turtle's egg. Told me that I had better watch it too. Apparently it's not only these poor cats and dogs they're blaming bing du on now, but migrant workers as well. "It's you waidi ren, outside people, who bring in diseases," he said.'

'Ai! Mrs A, its enough to make me want to wring his fat neck!'

Mrs A laid a hand on Auntie Li's shoulder. 'Ignore that thug. No one around here likes him much anyway. And not all the hutong folk are like him, Auntie. No one cares where you're from. I've seen you chat with the mahjong-playing lot that are always lounging outside Old Lady Fang's shop. You're quite a hit!'

Auntie Li smiled. 'Oh, I know not all city folk are painted with the same brush. I just get so angry with the likes of Fat Tao. By the way, Old Lady Fang's not doing too well either. Her little dog Eraser went missing last night as well. I told her about Tofu. She's terribly worried.

There've been reports of gangs armed with sticks landing up at people's homes and demanding that they hand over their pets. If the owners refuse they beat them and steal away the animals, carrying them off to goodness knows where. Lots of folk have stopped taking their dogs out for walks.'

'What's wrong with these ren?' raged Mrs A. 'What makes them want to attack innocent animals like that? I refuse to believe that they cannot understand the difference between wild civet cats that live in the jungles and domestic cats and dogs. I know there is some evidence that bing du comes from civet cats but even if it does you can hardly blame the animals, can you? It's clearly the fault of ren who trap and eat these wild animals simply because the meat is rare.'

Auntie Li sighed heavily. 'Sometimes I think ren only get exactly what they deserve.'

I was feeling too miserable to listen to any more of this conversation, so much of which I found hard to follow. All I knew was that I missed Tofu and wanted her back so much I was willing to go without breakfast for a week if necessary.

I crept away from the kitchen into the yard and found a pale beam of sunlight to lie in. Forget about a week, I would go without breakfast for a month if that would bring Tofu back, I thought to myself.

I began to imagine days and days without any food and without Tofu. Tears swam in my eyes even though I blinked furiously to keep them away. My heart felt as empty as my stomach.

'Psst,' a sharp hissing sound had me scrambling onto my haunches, hackles raised. My ears went rigid, cutting triangles in the air, as I looked around slowly.

'Psst, Soyabean! Over here,' a voice meowed out again.

It was a cat. How did it know my name?

A thin, scraggly fellow made his way down to the edge of the main pavilion's roof. I arched my back threateningly and glared at the intruder.

'Don't be afraid, it's only me, Tofu's Da Ger,' the cat said in a loud whisper. A big chunk of his right ear was missing but he held himself proudly. 'I saw what happened to her last night. She's in trouble. They've got her. But your Ba and me, we'll try our best to find her.'

I felt my legs give way as I sank to the floor in astonishment. So all of Tofu's stories about her Da Ge had been real. He did live nearby and did come around and he did know my Ba. How could I not have believed her? I was such an idiotic cat.

'I don't understand, Da Ge. What did you see last night? Who has got Tofu? And where is my Ba?' The questions came tumbling out.

'Soyabean, there are things it's better for a pet cat like you never to find out about. Ren are not all gentle and loving like your owners. They can be terribly cruel. A bad one got hold of Tofu last night.'

'They've been grabbing as many of us as they can recently. Tofu was lucky. Sometimes they kill the animals they catch on the spot. Bludgeon them with clubs or throw them out of windows. But Tofu was taken away in a van. It attracts less attention if they get rid of the animals somewhere far away. That way, the owners never find out and can't kick up a fuss.'

'But try not to worry about Tofu. I know my Number Three. She's a small cat but smart. She won't give up easily. I'm sure she must have escaped from that van. Your Ba and I will search the whole city for her, street by street if we have to and we'll find her, Soyabean. I promise you that.'

He broke off suddenly, sniffing at the air.

'Someone's coming,' he said urgently, 'I must go. But hang in there kid. Your Ba won't let you down.'

With a quick bound, Da Ge leapt across the roof and disappeared. I opened my mouth to ask more questions, but it was too late. He was no longer around to answer.

'I'm really not in the mood to entertain guests; and least of all Xiao Xu. He gives me the creeps,' Mrs A came out of the kitchen her hands wrapped around a large cup of tea.

'I told him about Tofu having disappeared and that we were all upset. But he was very insistent about wanting to visit,' Auntie Li replied, following Mrs A out. 'That Maomi Deluxe friend of his, Liu, will be coming too. They say they have some good news to share with you. But don't worry. It'll take them at least an hour to get here. Why don't you go have a nice, warm, shower and I'll prepare some snacks to serve.'

Mrs A nodded and made for the bathroom while Auntie Li went back inside the kitchen. Mr A was locked away in his study. In so many ways it seemed like any other day. But it wasn't. Tofu was gone.

She wasn't up in the pomegranate tree. She wasn't in the kitchen nudging her bowl of food over to me. She wasn't locked up in a cupboard by mistake, waiting for me to get Mrs A to let her out. She was gone and I felt her absence everywhere.

I wished Da Ge would come back so I could find

out more about what he knew. Who had taken away Tofu in a van? Had she been hurt? Where were they taking her? And what about my Ba?

The thought of my Ba brought back a flood of memories. Curling up against Ma's belly; Nai Nai's gentle hands stroking my chin; stalking dragonflies in the courtyard. I had been so young and foolish then, running around imagining myself big and brave. I missed Ma. And I missed Nai Nai. I felt all alone now.

Auntie Li had just said Xiao Xu and Liu Laoban would be coming over with some good news about Maomi Deluxe. That should have made me excited. But it didn't. I didn't feel like seeing Xiao Xu at all. And I didn't want to hear anything more about Maomi Deluxe. If it hadn't been for that ad, I would have noticed Tofu missing much earlier. And instead of being trapped in some horrible van, she would be here in the yard with me.

I sat at the foot of the tree for the next hour, hardly moving. A line of ants went crawling right past my nose but I didn't have the energy to chase after them. I didn't move even when a loud knock on the door broke out.

Auntie Li went to open up and led Xiao Xu and Liu Laoban to chairs out in the yard. 'Mrs A will be with you soon,' she said to them, 'take a seat.'

'No worries,' replied Xiao Xu, running his hand through his hair. 'We'll wait out here with our friend

Soyabean.' He turned towards me, clicking his fingers in summons, 'Maomi! Lai, lai! Come away from that tree? Come to Xiao Xu.' When I didn't get up he scowled and raised his voice.

'What's wrong with you today? Get over here.'

'Leave him alone. Soyabean is upset about Tofu. We all are,' said Auntie Li. She looked Liu Laoban up and down. 'I suppose you'd like some tea?' she asked. 'I'll go and get some.'

'Quite a place they've got here, these waiguo friends of yours,' Liu Laoban drawled lazily once Auntie Li had left for the kitchen. 'Who would have thought a palace like this would exist in the middle of a dirty hutong. That fat-cat Soyabean is lucky to have such rich owners.'

'That fatty is going to make you and me far richer than any waiguo ren,' replied Xiao Xu grinning widely. 'How much did you say Maomi Deluxe had increased its sales after the ad aired on TV?'

'Forty times more, my friend. Forty times more! Sales have been going through the roof, right up to the heavens. People love this maomi. We've been flooded with letters from all over the place asking about him. He's a star!'

'It's tough for anyone to resist buying our cat food after they watch him gobbling it up with the kind of enjoyment that cannot be faked. Your maomi loves our Maomi Deluxe or at least that's what anyone watching the ad comes away convinced of.'

When Liu Laoban smiled I could see his whole mouth was filled with rotting teeth. I couldn't understand it. I should have been bursting with happiness. I was famous. People thought I was great. And I was going to make everyone rich. But I only wanted to cry.

What was the value of money when it could so easily be used up? I heard Nai Nai's voice echo in my head. I remembered how she would always tell Xiao Xu: 'Fill your head rather than your pocket and you can never be robbed.'

How I wished I had been wiser. Wisdom would have helped save Tofu. But no amount of money could. Nai Nai had been right. What was the use of money without wisdom?

'Ku bi le! That's too cool!' chuckled Xiao Xu. 'But there's no need to tell these waiguo ren exactly how much profit we end up making, right? I guess we'll have to shell out some cash to them but let's keep quiet on the details.'

'Anyway, they're so stupid I don't think they even care that much about the money. Apparently they're so upset about that flea-bitten black cat of theirs having vanished that they didn't want to see us! Not even when I said I had good news on the Maomi Deluxe front. Too busy moping around over their darling little Tofu.'

Xiao Xu snorted loudly before continuing. 'It's amazing how these ren care more about their cats than human beings. Anyway, I believe if you're dumb enough to be cheated then you deserve to be cheated. So let's just keep the numbers small. Tell them the cat food's selling well and hand over some small change. I doubt they'll ask too many questions. Probably, they'll just go and spend the money on more food for their cats!'

Liu Laoban roared with laughter. 'That's the beauty of it,' he said slapping his thigh. 'People waste their money on these good-for-nothing cats and it only makes us richer. Look at all these fools spending a small fortune on Maomi Deluxe. I swear, this is the sweetest business I've ever had. Fifty cents to produce a box of food you can sell for 15 Yuan. Can't beat that, can you, ge menr?'

Xiao Xu went quiet. An odd glint flitted across his eyes as he leant forward towards Liu Laoban.

'But tell me something Laoban,' he asked, his voice barely above a whisper. I had to lift open my ears fully to catch what he was saying.

'How do you do it? How can you make so much profit? How can it only cost 50 cents to make something that sells for 15 Yuan. Come on, boss-man, what trick are you keeping hidden away in your brocade bag? I know you're a crafty fox.'

Xiao Xu's mouth was glistening with spit, his faced mottled with greed.

Liu Laoban leant forward as well, until his head was almost touching Xiao Xu's. 'The answer ge menr, lies in one word.' He paused for a second and looked around as if to make sure they were alone in the yard.

Xiao Xu's eyes had grown so huge they looked as if they would burst out of his face. One word?' he breathed with excitement. 'What word, Laoban?'

'Protein,' replied Liu Loaban smugly. 'The key is protein.'

'Protein?' repeated Xiao Xu, looking startled? 'Whatever do you mean?'

'Oh you stupid melon!' laughed Liu Laoban. 'Don't you know anything? It's simple. The higher the protein content in pet food the more nutritious it is and the more you can charge for it. But, and here lies the catch, protein is also what makes pet food expensive.'

He pulled away from Xiao Xu and relaxed back in his chair. 'So, make the protein cheap and you can make the food cheap but sell it at a high price nonetheless. Simple!'

'But you just said that protein was expensive,' said Xiao Xu. He was looking very excited. 'So how do you make something that's expensive, cheaply?' Liu Laoban raised his eyebrows and was about to reply when Mrs A came out of the main pavilion, walking quickly.

'Ni hao Xiao Xu,' she said. 'I'm sorry to have kept you waiting but we've had a slow start today. We were up late last night looking for Tofu. Have you had something to eat?' Her eyes were puffy but she was smiling in a determined way.

Auntie Li appeared with a plate of snacks and a pot of tea. Everyone helped themselves from a bowl of sunflower seeds Auntie Li put out on the table. Mrs A made some comment about the weather, the favourite topic of Ren.

I found myself unable to pay attention. My mind was running so fast I felt breathless. I hadn't liked what I'd overheard at all. It smelt of rotten eggs. What was all this about a protein? I didn't know what a protein was but I knew that something expensive couldn't suddenly become something cheap.

And the way in which Xiao Xu had called Tofu a flea-bitten, dumb cat! He didn't care about her at all. What's more, I was realizing that he didn't care about me either. All those treats he used to bring me, they were just bribes. He only wanted to use me to make money. And he was even planning to cheat Mr and Mrs A of their share!

I felt the blood rush to my head.

'I'm busy with real estate projects these days,' Xiao Xu was telling Mrs A chattily. 'As you know, China will be hosting the big Games soon and we need to make sure that Beijing is ready. When the world's eyes are on us, we will show them a new city, a modern city, a rich city.'

'My friend Mr Liu here is one of China's most successful businessmen.'

Liu Laoban gave Mrs A an oily smile. I felt my claws come unsheathed.

'Cat food is just a side-business for him. His real interests are in construction. In fact he's building a block of luxury apartments right by the Games Village. It will be top-end stuff,' Xiao Xu went on. 'That's the kind of place you should be living in. Not some mouldy old hutong, like this. It smells like one big toilet out here. Totally unsuitable for waiguo ren. Bring your husband and come take a look at our building site when you have some time.'

I couldn't bear to hear a single word more. Before I knew what I was doing I was flying across the courtyard, hurtling towards Xiao Xu.

As I sank my teeth deep into his thigh I felt happier than I had all day.

chapter eight

TOFU

Black Cat, White Cat

The van was tearing along so fast that every time it took a turn we found ourselves collapsing into a big heap. Tails and whiskers intertwined. Meows and barks crashed into each other. Eraser was pressed up close to me and I could feel his heartbeat galloping, matching mine.

Where were we going?

The narrow window along the back door was high up and it was difficult to look out. Street lamps rushed by in a blur. Inside the van a kitten was mewling non-stop. I wanted to hold it close and lick away its tears but I couldn't find my way to it in the crush.

Many of the animals had been hurt while being shoved into the van. The sticky smell of blood filled the space. I wanted to throw up but forced myself to clear my head. I knew I needed to be clever and quick if I were going to escape.

All of a sudden, I was thrown to one side. Several animals cried out as their bodies smashed up against the walls of the van. We had come to an abrupt stop.

'Open up!' 'Open up at once!'

A banging broke out on the doors.

Eraser and I looked at each other, our eyes wide. What was going on? Why had we stopped? Who were the Ren outside banging on the van?

We heard the front door opening and someone getting out. I stretched my ears as far open as I could to hear what was going on.

'Who are you lot? What right do you have to surround my vehicle like this? Clear off at once!'

I immediately recognized the low drawl of the Ren who had kidnapped me. The bruises his long fingernails had left along my belly were still hot and painful.

Outside a deafening clamour arose. It sounded like a thick crowd of Ren. I couldn't make out what anyone was saying, it was all so noisy. Then everything quieted down and a woman's voice rang clear.

'We are members of the Capital Animal Welfare Association. We have it on good authority that you and your friends have been illegally kidnapping and murdering pets. Open up the back of this vehicle immediately. We want to see what you are hiding away there. You murderer!'

The voice sounded strangely familiar but before I had any time to puzzle over this the banging on the doors restarted.

'Open up! Murderer! Open up! Murderer!' the crowd began to chant.

'Keep away from my car, you melon-heads! There's nothing back there. You have no right!' But the man's voice was drowned out by the others. We could hear thuds and kicks. The back door began to rattle as the crowd tried to break in.

'Cry out as loudly as you can!' the deep woof of the Cai Gou urged everyone. 'Meow and bark and growl and yelp. Let them know we are inside.' A tremendous din filled the van as the animals obeyed. I joined in although my meows were too soft to make a real difference. The crowd outside responded by battering the van with even greater vigour.

'They're inside! Can you hear them? Break down the door. Free our innocent friends.' It was the familiar voice again.

Gradually the door began to cave in. I knew that this was the one chance I had of getting myself out of this mess. If I could keep my wits about me and run for it the moment the door was forced open, Da Ge would find me. He would take me home to Mrs A and Soyabean. I would be back where I belonged and this whole nightmare would be over. I just had to stay focussed.

But as I was getting ready for the moment of escape, the attack on the van died down. An argument between the Ren outside seemed to have broken out.

'Move away from the van. How can you love animals more than human beings? Don't you know these filthy creatures are spreading the awful disease that's killing everyone?' a new high-pitched voice screeched.

'The animals aren't the ones who are filthy. Its human beings like you who slaughter helpless creatures who can't speak for themselves. You are the ones who are sick. Even more sick than those who have bing du because you enjoy inflicting pain,' the familiar voice replied.

There was something about that voice. It reminded me of another time; a time when I knew little of the World except from Mama's stories. It took me back to my kitten-hood, playing with my brothers in Old Man Zhao's garden.

In a flash it came to me.

The voice was Madam Wang's; the cat protection society Ren who had led Mr and Mrs A to me. Barely a second after I was able to place the voice, the doors crashed open. The dozen animals behind me surged forward and I found myself propelled into a crowd of strange Ren standing outside.

I felt Ren breath sweeping over me, Ren hands reaching out to grab me. Someone caught me by the tail. I yelped in pain. Someone else began to slap the Ren who was holding on to me, on the head.

'Let the cat go you uncivilized brute!'

It was Madam Wang.

'Ai! You crazy, animal-loving freak,' the Ren shouted back. But he loosened his grip on my tail and I was away. Only one thought played in my head over and over again: Da Ge calling out after me, urging me to run.

And so I ran, without glancing left or right. All I knew was that I had to get away; from the Ren, from the van, from the shouting and banging. I ran and ran until I felt my chest would burst and even then I kept running. I had no idea where I was going but it was dark and quiet and there were no Ren in sight. That was good enough for me.

'Tofu. Wait! Wait for me,' a panting yelp came from behind. I swung around, my tail rigid with alarm, but it was only Eraser. The dog looked in bad shape. He was wheezing hard and red patches of skin were showing through on his neck where bits of hair had been torn out.

'Don't leave me alone in the night, please Tofu,' Eraser said as he leant against a wall to catch his breath. 'You said everything would be okay. You said your Da Ge would find us and take us home. But then you ran away like that. Where are you going? Aren't you going to take me with you?'

Eraser had collapsed heaving into a heap and even

in the dark I could make out the shiny tears running down his face.

I immediately went up to him and rubbed my cheek against his side. 'Don't cry Eraser,' I said licking his face. 'I wasn't running away from you. I just needed to get away. I don't like Ren very much, you know, apart from Mr and Mrs A, and maybe Auntie Li. And I don't like fighting and noise.'

Eraser was calming down; his breathing becoming more regular.

'I wasn't leaving you behind. I just wasn't thinking clearly,' I continued. 'We'll stick together Eraser. We'll be home in no time. Da Ge will find us.'

I don't know at what point exactly but we must have fallen asleep. The rain had finally stopped and the wind died down. And even though it was damp we were able to keep warm by cuddling up close. I could never have imagined it: a cat like me and Old Lady Fang's yappy little dog lying together like litter-mates.

The next morning, the rays of the rising sun pricked my still-closed eyelids. I could feel Eraser shifting next to me but the image of Mrs A scratching my ears while I lay on her lap lingered.

Morning? Eraser? Where was I? What was going on?

I sat bolt upright; cozy dreams replaced by cold reality. We were lost. My body hurt. My eyes burned. I was hungry. How would Da Ge know where to find us? My tail felt heavy with despair. And then I saw it.

It rose out of the earth like a gigantic, glinting, nest; so huge I couldn't see where it began and where it ended. Its centre yawned empty and wide like a hungry, toothless mouth. It was surrounded by cranes and big machines with metallic arms and jagged hooks. A haze of dust hung over the whole scene.

Looking up at it I felt smaller than I ever had before. How could anything be so large? Even thousands and thousands of cats put together wouldn't be enough to fill it up. But what in the World was it?

'So, that's the famous Stadium.' Eraser was up and staring transfixed at the building.

'What's the Stadium? And how do *you* know this is it?' I asked, a tad snappily. My stomach was making growling noises. And to find little Eraser suddenly so knowledgeable was irritating.

'Old Lady Fang's always talking about it,' he said still unable to tear his gaze away.

'She has a photograph of it up in her room. It's being built for something called the big Games and when it's ready many waiguo Ren from far away will come and run around inside it.'

I had no idea what Eraser was talking about. It sounded quite crazy. Why would Ren build something so huge and complicated just to run inside of? Perhaps Eraser had misheard his mistress.

Seeing my disbelieving expression, the dog became

quite sulky. He stuck his lower lip out and hung his head low.

'You don't believe me, do you Tofu?' he asked. 'But it's true. Really! Old Lady Fang's cousin is one of the Ren building this Stadium. He's from a tiny village in Dongbei, away in the northeast. Many thousands of Ren have come from villages all over China to make this building, let me tell you.'

'It's costing a lot of money too. Old Lady Zhao's always complaining about how the government is ready to spend so much on the big Games but won't build a proper toilet in the hutong for Ren to use.'

The dog seemed to know so much that I felt almost hopeful. 'Eraser, do you know where in Beijing this Stadium is? Is it far from our hutong? Do you know how to get home from it?' I asked.

But Eraser shook his head. 'I've never been here before Tofu. I've never been anywhere really. The furthest Old Lady Fang ever takes me is for a walk to the bottom of the hutong. She doesn't have a dog license for me, you see. She's afraid the police will take me away if they find out.'

I could see the tears coming back to Eraser's eyes. 'She'll be so worried about me. And she has a weak heart, you know.'

'I know, I know,' I said quickly, trying to think of something to distract him.

'Are you hungry?' I asked. It was the first thing that popped into my head. The growling in my stomach had been becoming louder. Eraser immediately looked interested. 'Yes,' he barked excitedly. 'I'm starving. Can you catch us some food?'

'Me?' I asked. 'How?'

'What do you mean "how"?' replied Eraser testily. 'You're a cat aren't you? Can't you catch a rat or something? I thought that's what you cats do.'

'Can you see any rats strolling around waiting to be caught?' I retorted, my whiskers quivering with irritation. 'And as far as I'm aware a dog is as capable as a cat when it comes to catching them. Or are they too stupid to?'

Eraser's eyes grew dangerously wet as he struggled to answer. I felt bad for having made him cry. This was no time for trading insults. Eraser was the only one I could count on out here. He may have been a silly, little dog, but he was my friend. I needed to look after him. Dogs weren't very bright after all.

'Right,' I said briskly before he could start bawling. 'Food! We need to find some dustbins.'

I had never thought I would be grateful for my time as a dustbin cat, but it was training that was useful in this situation. I hadn't ever had to scavenge for food myself but I remembered Mama's stories of her foraging expeditions. Dustbins were always the best source of eatable scraps.

As we searched we wandered closer and closer to the Stadium building site. The hammering noise from the machines was quite terrifying but I knew that where there were machines, there were Ren to make them work and where there were Ren there was sure to be food.

The ache in my stomach was becoming heavy, like a stone. I wondered whether Mama had often felt like this. Where was she now? Was she hungry like me?

'My stomach hurts Tofu,' Eraser moaned. We were hiding behind a mound of earth that a claw-like machine kept adding more soil to. Poofs of dust flew into the sky every few seconds. Eraser was covered in grit; his white fur had turned brown.

'Where are the dustbins? Where is the food?' the dog asked for the millionth time. Even though the sun was quite high by now, we hadn't had much luck finding anything to eat. The area was one big building site and it didn't look like anyone lived there. I hadn't been able to spot a single dustbin so far.

The Ren scurrying around were also different to any I had met before. They looked funny; thinner and darker. They smelt different; stinkier and sweatier. Their teeth were stained and cracked. They spoke with accents that were difficult to understand.

Eraser said it was because they came from far away villages. 'These are Nongmin Gong, migrant workers, like Old Lady Fang's cousin,' he whispered.

'Why do they look like this?' I asked.

'It's because they are very poor and have to work very hard and don't get enough to eat. Whenever Old

Lady Fang's cousin comes to visit he eats enough to last him for week.'

A long time passed before the machines finally fell still and the Ren took a break to eat. Instead of sitting down on tables with chairs like in the As' home, they just squatted on their haunches. Like cats.

They shovelled food into their mouths from plastic trays, hardly bothering to chew. 'Stay here,' I hissed at Eraser.

Although I was scared, I knew that one of us had to come out of hiding to try and scrounge scraps off the Ren. My mouth was flooding with saliva at the though of food, any kind of food.

How I wished Soyabean were here. He was so much braver than me. But I only had Eraser and I was quite sure he wasn't up to the task. Dogs! It would have to be me. Taking a deep breath, I crept out from behind the mound as silently as I could. Almost immediately I found myself looking straight into a Ren's eyes.

His mouth hung open in surprise and I could see bits of rice in there. I tensed, ready to bolt in a flash if necessary. But the Ren didn't move. Nor did I. I'm not sure how long passed before the Ren slowly moved his chopsticks into his tray, picked up some food and then put it out on the floor, right in front of me.

I didn't know what to do. I was so hungry that part

of me just wanted to jump on the food and gobble it down without any further thought. But I held back. Could I trust this Ren? Was this just an attempt to lure me closer? Would he hurt me? I felt the panic rise in my throat.

But then I saw the way in which the Ren was looking at me: still, curious, gentle. He was a small man and his clothes were torn and filthy. He was sweating. The sun was directly overhead and there was no shelter.

I took one step forward cautiously. The Ren remained still. I took another step. Then I stopped. The Ren extended his chopsticks and nudged the morsel of food even closer to me.

I couldn't wait any longer. In a moment I had swallowed it up. I wasn't sure what it was and it was cold at that, but it tasted better than the most tender pieces of chicken liver Auntie Li served hot off the stove.

The Ren smiled widely. It made him look quite handsome even though his face was black with the sun and dirt. He put out another bit of food from his tray. I ate it. It was only when he offered up a third mouthful that I remembered Eraser.

I ran back to our hiding place and motioned to the dog to follow me. When I remerged along with him, the Ren was still out there, squatting in the same position. He laughed out loud when he saw us and then emptied out half his tray for us to eat.

We fell upon the food and polished it off quickly. We looked up. The Ren was standing over us. 'I'm sorry but that's all I have to offer you two,' he said, scratching his chin slowly. He sighed loudly.

'You poor things! You look so scared. Are you lost?' He ran his hand through his hair and I noticed how he had only four fingers on his right hand.

'The world's not made for the likes of us eh?' he continued. 'We're the ones who do all the work but we stay as poor as alley cats, while the fat cat big shots get richer and fatter making fancy stadiums and selling fancy houses.'

He bent down to tickle me behind the ears. It felt unusual because he had a finger missing, but I was strangely unafraid. This Ren would not hurt me. I sensed this.

'Ai maomi!' he sighed. 'Our great leader Deng Xiaoping said it didn't matter if it was a black cat or white cat as long as it caught mice. But he forgot to add that what really matters is whether it's a rich cat or a poor cat. You see there are no mice to catch for the peasant cat at all. The fat cats in the city gobble them all up, leaving nothing for the rest.'

Eraser nudged me with his nose. 'I'm a bit confused, Tofu. Is he really talking about cats?' Dogs just weren't very bright.

'No Eraser I think what he's saying is that like there are dustbin cats and spoilt pets, there are dustbin-Ren and other, rich-Ren,' I whispered back.

I felt sad. This was such a nice Ren and yet he must have a very hard life. Like Mama. Why were some Ren born unlucky and some lucky? It didn't seem fair.

'Well, my new friends,' the Ren continued, 'I'm very pleased to have made your acquaintance. And I'll come looking for you later. But I have to get back to work and you had better go back to your hiding place. There's folk here so hungry they'll catch you to cook and eat for dinner.'

Eraser's ears immediately flattened, but the Ren gave us a slow wink. Was he making a joke? I supposed he must have been. But then I remembered Mama telling me that there really are Ren out there who eat cats and I wasn't wholly convinced the Ren was only joking.

chapter nine

SOYABEAN

No Wave Without Wind

Mrs A had been sulking with me ever since I'd bitten Xiao Xu. She said she couldn't understand how I could have hurt anyone. 'I don't know you anymore,' she sighed with a sad, disappointed mouth. I felt smaller than a dragonfly when she looked at me like that.

For the first time in my life I found myself unable to communicate with her. No matter how much I meowed I couldn't explain to her that it was Xiao Xu who was bad. That he'd been cheating us all along. I remembered how I used to show off to Tofu about being able to talk with Ren. But in fact I was no good even at that. I was truly the most useless cat in the World.

It had been several days since Da Ge had come

around to tell me about what had happened to Tofu and there was still no news of her. I kept waiting, hoping he would come back with more information but he never did. I spent whole afternoons peering at the rooftops but all I could see was the blank blue sky; no Da Ge, no Ba, no Tofu.

The pomegranate fruit on the tree in the yard had shrivelled up and the leaves had mostly fallen off. The tree looked smaller, shabbier; like I felt myself.

The Maomi Deluxe ad was on TV all the time. I felt like scratching the TV set every time it came on. I hated the ad. And I hated myself for having done it and fallen straight into Xiao Xu's trap. We hadn't heard anything from him or Liu Laoban since the day I'd bitten him.

My whiskers still danced in satisfaction when I remembered the way Xiao Xu had howled in pain after I'd scraped the skin off his thigh. He'd left in a hurry afterwards, glaring at me threateningly and muttering darkly under his breath.

But I hadn't backed down. I had glared right back, snarling as fiercely as I could. 'Soyabean!' Mrs A had said her voice choking with reproach. I wished so much that I could make her understand.

The only good news was that the bing du virus seemed to be under control. Auntie Li no longer wore a face mask when she came to work in the mornings.

That evening I heard Mr A saying that the virus

was not a big problem any more. 'See I was right,' he said to Mrs A holding up a newspaper. They were sitting around the kitchen table while Auntie Li prepared dinner. 'No new cases of the virus are being reported and the total number of people infected in all Beijing is only about 2,000.'

'It's going to blow over like I've been saying throughout. A week with no new cases and everyone will calm down.'

'That may be, but it's a bit late for Tofu, isn't it,' Mrs A snapped back. Her voice was high-pitched. She'd had swollen eyes ever since Tofu had disappeared. 'It won't help Tofu will it, if everyone goes back to pretending that everything is hunky dory and that nothing noteworthy ever happened? That they hadn't gone crazy, kidnapping animals, doing who knows what to them.'

Mrs A let out an airless sob. Mr A looked blankly at the newspaper he was holding out. His shoulders were slack, defeated. But Auntie Li went up to her and gave her a quick hug.

'Don't lose hope Tai Tai,' she said. 'You never know. Tofu might still turn up one of these days. Stranger things have happened.

'It's funny you say that,' Mrs A gave a quick, little laugh. But it was a false laugh, without real happiness. 'That's exactly what Madam Wang said to me.'

'Who is Madam Wang?' asked Auntie Li, scrunching up her nose.

'Madam Wang? That's the lady who helped us find Tofu. She runs a cat protection society up at one of the university campuses and we'd contacted her when we were looking to adopt a kitten. She had some old professor friend with a litter in his backyard and that's where we found Tofu.'

'When did you speak to her?' asked Mr A turning around on his stool to face her.

'Just this morning. She called me out of the blue to ask if she could come and visit. Something odd about wanting to discuss Maomi Deluxe. Quite mystifying really, but she wouldn't say more.'

'I was so ashamed to confess that we'd lost Tofu!' sighed Mrs A. 'After all the promises we'd made her. "Don't worry Madam Wang, we'll take excellent care of little Tofu." We've failed so badly. I feel so guilty.'

There was a silence in the kitchen. Mr A rubbed his eyes tiredly. I felt what had become a familiar feeling of depression wrap around me. Eventually Mr A cleared his throat.

'Well, how did she take it? What did she say,' he asked.

'It was odd. She seemed almost unsurprised,' replied Mrs A. 'In fact she was rather sweet and didn't sound reproachful at all. Just said she would come by tomorrow morning to see us.'

That night I stayed outside in the yard even though it was getting quite cold. I could no longer bring myself to sleep in the As' bedroom like I used to, lying comfortably on smooth silk sheets while Tofu was out there in the World, all on her own.

Sometimes an icy thought cut its way into my head. What if she wasn't out there anymore at all? But I just couldn't bring myself to believe it. She must have escaped from that van. She must have.

The night stretched on and on, getting colder and darker. There was no sign of Da Ge. I curled up into a ball on the window sill outside the study, feeling the shadow of the pomegranate tree weigh on me like a pile of bricks.

It was almost noon the next day when Madam Wang finally showed up at the house. She entered the courtyard briskly, carrying her bicycle with her. 'Where can I put this?' she asked Mrs A, who had let her in.

'Oh! Just park it in that corner,' Mrs A pointed towards the study.

'Ai! It's cold today,' said Madam Wang as she put down her bicycle. She had young, bright eyes, even though the skin around them was wrinkled. 'Beijing is no longer the city it used to be,' she continued, taking off her jacket. 'So many cars on the road now. And the pollution! I can barely breathe anymore when I'm cycling.'

'You waiguo ren may not know it, but there was a time when a bicycle commanded respect in this city. Now of course it's all about money. Who is making it. How much they are making. What kind of car they can afford. That's all that seems to matter now.'

'It's become a third-rate place, this city. Tai keqi le! It's such a pity!'

'You know, my daughter's always going on about how I should buy a car. But what use do I have for one? "You're too old to ride a bicycle," she tells me. But even the old horse in the stable yearns to run a 1,000 li, or so they say!'

Mrs Wang let out a loud, hearty laugh. 'And besides I feel like the longer I live, the more energy I have!'

'You certainly look in great shape Madam Wang,' said Mrs A smiling politely, as she led Madam Wang to the living room. 'Your hair is so black.'

'Oh that?' she replied plopping down on a sofa. 'That's just hair dye.'

Mrs A looked flustered and busied herself with pouring out a cup of tea. I leapt up onto the sofa and sat snuggled next to her. For the first time in days, she didn't shove me away. Had she finally forgiven me for biting Xiao Xu?

'Mrs A,' said Madam Wang leaning forward to accept the tea-cup. 'There's something I want to tell you. I didn't mention anything yesterday because I didn't want to give you false hope. But you should know this. It's about Tofu.'

Mrs A's head swung up.

'Tofu? What is it Madam Wang? What do you want to tell me,' she asked, the words all tumbling into each other.

Madam Wang took a slow sip of tea before replying.

'Well, ten days ago, around the same time you say Tofu vanished, I was out on the streets with other members of the Capital Animal Welfare Association and I think I might have spotted your cat.'

I could feel Mrs A go rigid.

'What do you mean? Where? How?' she asked. Her hand played at her neck nervously. My heart was also racing. What exactly had this Madam Wang seen?

'Now, don't get overexcited Mrs A, but that night—I remember it well because it was raining so hard—I was out patrolling the streets with my group of animal rights activists. We've been doing this almost every night following tip offs from pet owners. So many little ones have been carried off by these brutish, anti-bing du mobs.'

'Now, that night we surrounded a white van we believed to be carrying a number of animals that had been kidnapped. It was just a few kilometers north of here, near the Stadium for the Games.'

'We were able to break open the back door and, sure enough, several animals came rushing out. But although we managed to rescue a few, some panicked and got away.'

Mrs A was so still I couldn't even feel her breathe. As for me, I was breathing so fast I felt full to bursting with air. 'Was Tofu amongst those that escaped, Madam Wang?' asked Mrs A, slowly. Her voice was as thin as paper.

'All I can say for sure is that I could swear that one looked an awful lot like your Tofu,' she replied. 'But you must also keep in mind that I haven't seen Tofu since she was a skinny, little kitten. I could have been mistaken.'

'On the other hand,' she continued, 'Tofu's mother still lives on our college campus. Do you remember Old Man Zhao, the retired professor? Tofu was born in the dustbin in his back yard?'

Mrs A nodded quickly.

'He had a heart attack poor soul and was in hospital for a long while. But he's back home now and he's taken the mother in, to live with him as a pet. His wife died years ago and he's very lonely. Doesn't have many friends. So the cat is a great comfort to him.'

'Madam Wang, was that Tofu you saw?' asked Mrs A again, more roughly than was usual for her.

'That's just what I was trying to tell you, dear. I see the mother quite often. Whenever I visit Old Man Zhao. And the cat I saw coming out of the van we stopped that night had a definite resemblance to her. It's a real possibility it was Tofu I saw, Mrs A, but in all honesty I can't 100 per cent guarantee it.'

I thumped my tail up and down. I wanted to vault up all the way up to the room's ceiling, I was so thrilled. Tofu had escaped! It must have been her Madam Wang saw that night. I was certain of it.

And if she was out free, then no matter where she

was, my Ba and Da Ge would find her. I felt the lump I had been carrying around in my throat begin to melt and for the first time in days a small hunger pang pinged in my belly.

But Mrs A remained stony faced. 'Madam Wang, thank you for coming over to tell me this. It gives me some hope but the truth is that even if it was Tofu that night I'm not sure she would have survived all these days on her own with no one to feed her or comfort her. You see, she's such a little cat,' Mrs A's voice began to crack.

Madam Wang took another long sip of tea before speaking. 'Mrs A, don't underestimate your Tofu. She might be small but she comes from tough stock. If she has any of her mother's genes in her she could well surprise you.'

She put her tea-cup down in front of her and settled back on the sofa cushions. 'Look, I must also tell you that I didn't come over today only to discuss Tofu. There's also this matter of Maomi Deluxe and your other maomi, the famous Soyabean.'

Madam Wang turned to give me a tickle behind the ears. Her fingers smelt of soap. Mrs A who had been staring at her hands as if she'd never seen them before, looked up.

'Oh yes. You had mentioned something about that on the phone. What is it?'

Madam Wang kept up the tickling. Funnily enough, it made me feel quite peckish. When was the last time I had sat down to eat a really proper meal? I couldn't even remember. Some hot chicken bits would hit the spot, I found myself thinking.

'What a handsome fellow he is, your Soyabean. So golden and fluffy.' Madam Wang was working my ears expertly. She was a very good tickler. I purred in appreciation, perhaps a trifle more loudly than was polite, but it really was good stuff.

'I was just wondering,' continued Madam Wang, 'if Soyabean's been feeling well lately? Any vomiting? Stomach pains?'

Mrs A raised her eyebrows in surprise. 'He's been a bit depressed about Tofu having disappeared. They were very fond of each other. But he hasn't been ill or anything. Although his appetite's a bit smaller than normal.'

Mrs A paused to look me up and down. 'Given his size, perhaps that's just as well! Why do you ask?'

Madam Wang was looking at me intently. 'Hmm,' she murmured as if unsatisfied with the answer. But then she sat back on the sofa once again and smiled good naturedly.

'It's probably nothing. Just that several of my cat protection society members have begun to report a mysterious illness in their cats. Vomiting, diarrhea, that kind of thing. And now there have even been a few cases of kidney failure.' She paused.

Mrs A nodded, encouraging her to go on.

'The strange thing is what all these sick cats have

had in common is that their owners recently started feeding them Maomi Deluxe. You know it's quite an expensive brand and many of our members can ill afford it. But it's supposed to be high in nutrition and of course your Soyabean is so persuasive in the ad, that many have started buying it regardless of the price.'

'That's why I thought of visiting you. To ask if he'd been sick as well. But since you say not, I suppose Maomi Deluxe couldn't be the culprit after all.'

'Strange though, don't you think? As we say in China, there's no wave without a wind. But I've not even been able to detect a light breeze yet. I guess I'll have to just keep looking.'

Madam Wang stood up to take her leave. 'Well, I must be going. Thank you so much for receiving me today. And don't give up on little Tofu just . . .'

My agitated meows interrupted her mid-sentence. I stood up on my hind legs and pulled at her trousers with my front paws. 'Soyabean?' she asked bending down towards me, concern in her voice. 'What's wrong?'

Cats were getting sick after eating Maomi Deluxe. It must have something to do with the protein that Liu Laoban had mentioned. Maomi Deluxe was the wind causing the wave. I didn't know exactly how, but I did know that Xiao Xu and his friends were up to no good with that cat food.

Everything was my fault. If only I had never done

the ad. If only I had listened to Tofu. I had to find a way of explaining all this to Madam Wang and Mrs A. But how? My meows were just that to them—useless, meaningless sounds.

'Oh ignore him,' Mrs A said to Madam Wang, shaking her head. 'He's been acting very peculiarly lately. I don't know what's wrong with him.'

chapter ten

TOFU

Dustbin Ren

I woke up with a headache. It had been like this every day since we'd come to live in the migrant worker Four Fingers Fu's shack. I had a headache and a bellyache, but most of all a heartache.

I wasn't sure how long it had been. The days melted into one another. Perhaps a week? Or a month? The nights were very long now and my fur was growing longer. It bunched up into knotty tangles. Auntie Li was no longer around to brush my coat and although Four Fingers Fu was a kind Ren, he barely brushed his own hair, let alone mine or Eraser's.

I don't know what we would have done without him, though. He fed us and petted us and kept us going. We still didn't know much about him except a few things we'd picked up from overheard conversations between the Ren who lived in his shack. He was from a village in the far north where it was even colder and drier than Beijing. He had a wife and two daughters to whom he sent the money he earned building the Stadium.

He'd lost his little finger in an accident at work many years ago. A machine had sliced it off and gobbled it up. It was true what Da Ge had said to me, machines had no feelings. It was because they didn't have a heart. Sometimes I wished I didn't either. It would hurt so much less then.

That first night Four Fingers Fu came to our hiding place behind the mound of dirt to look for us, I had almost decided not to follow him. His comment about there being folk hungry enough to eat cats kept ringing in my ears. What if he was one of them? It didn't seem likely but Mama had always said you couldn't trust Ren.

In the end we didn't really have a choice. The sky had turned a stormy grey with great scowling clouds thrashing around in it. It would rain again that night. Eraser and I were both already exhausted from the previous evening and the prospect of another night out in the World was too much to bear.

The Ren—at the time we didn't even know his name—called out for us to go with him. He walked at a brisk pace and we had to trot quite fast to keep up. We circled around the enormous Stadium until we

finally came to a series of huts with tin roofs pushed up against the outer boundary wall of the construction site.

The Ren entered one of them, bent over in half because the roof was so low and beckoned for us to follow. I hesitated. 'Tofu, what should we do?' whispered Eraser, his whiskers quivering with anxiety. I took a deep breath and padded in through the door.

It felt like I had crashed into a wall of bad smells; the stench of cigarette smoke, sweaty bodies and unwashed feet. Later I was to realise that this was how being poor smelt. It was the stink of dustbin Ren.

A single, naked light bulb lit the shack. I could make out maybe seven or eight slab-like beds piled one on top of the other. A few Ren sat on the lower beds, smoking and playing cards. Others were sprawled out on the filthy floor.

'Well, well, look what Four Fingers Fu's brought for supper,' drawled one of the Ren from the floor. It was too dark to make out his face but he was clutching a bottle in his hand.

Eraser let out a low whine. My stomach fell to my paws. We were done for! It had been a trap and we'd walked right into it.

But Four Fingers Fu only chuckled. He took off his jacket and threw it at the Ren on the floor. 'You leave these two alone Old Zhu. They're as hungry and tired as any of us. Think of them as four-legged comrades.'

Then he turned to Eraser and me. We cowered as close to the ground as we could get.

'And you two. Don't pay any attention to Old Zhu. He's just a drunk fool. Prefers a liquid diet in any case, so you're quite safe from him!' The room erupted in laughter. I could hear someone cough up phlegm and spit it out.

A hulking, tall Ren got off from the top of a bunk bed and made directly for us. As his shadow blotted out the light from the bulb, I thought of Mama and Da Ge and Soyabean and Mrs A. I would never see them again.

I closed my eyes shut as tightly as I could and waited. I could hear Eraser whimpering faintly next to me. I felt bad that I'd fed him all those false promises of hope. We were never going to get home. This was the end.

A few seconds went by and then a few more. I kept my eyes shut. My heart was hammering as loudly as the machines constructing the Stadium. But nothing happened. No fatal blow or kick. Only a faint tickling in my whiskers. I finally found the courage to crack an eye open and found myself staring at two, thick fingers. They were unwashed and caked in dirt but they didn't seem threatening.

The tall Ren was holding them out under my nose. I felt weak with relief. He wanted to stroke me, that was all. 'I had me a tiny maomi when I was a child,' he said finally, petting me gently on the head. 'She was the sweetest thing and I took real good care of her. But then the great Chairman Mao decided we were all to give up farming and make steel in our backyards instead.'

The room filled with murmurs. 'That was a crazy time,' Four Fingers Fu said. 'Total chaos, da luan.'

'There was the famine,' the tall Ren continued. 'Days went by when all I ate in an entire day was a few grains of rice. We were a large family you see; seven children and we were starving. Later when all the remaining rice was gone, we began eating dirt mixed in water.

Then one day my little maomi disappeared. I cried and cried and spent all afternoon looking for her but she was nowhere to be found. That night we had meat for dinner for the first time in months.'

The shack had gone very still. All the Ren seemed to be holding their breath.

'When it was my turn to be served I screamed. And my Ma, she just slapped me hard and shouted at me to eat. "Eat!" she screamed, tears running down her face, and in the end I was so hungry I ate.'

I felt a few drops of wetness fall on my head. The tall Ren was crying. Beside me Eraser was sniffing. The entire room felt damp. I shivered. Finally Four Fingers Fu walked up to the tall Ren and put his hand on his shoulder.

'Lao Li, what's the use of thinking of the past? A happy childhood is a gift for the rich. Not for the likes of us. But we've got cigarettes and beer and each other; the poor man's gifts. Come, let's play a game of cards.'

Lao Li gave my head a final stroke before following Four Fingers Fu back to the bed where a group of Ren were sitting clutching torn cards.

There was a sameness to the days that followed. We spent the daylight hours out on the construction site amidst the grainy dust and pounding noise; and the nights squatting in the gloomy, crowded shack with the dustbin Ren and their sad stories.

Eraser was always hungry but I had no appetite. I found it hard to swallow even the few bits of rice and stringy vegetables Four Fingers Fu could spare for us. It kept me alive, though. The food and the thought that one day Da Ge would rescue me. I had no idea how far away from Ghost Street we were but my brother wouldn't give up. I knew he would scour every alley in Beijing to find me if necessary. It was only a matter of time.

'When will Da Ge come, Tofu?' Eraser always asked me at night before he went to sleep. 'Soon Eraser, soon,' I would murmur. 'It's only a matter of time.' The poor dog. He was so skinny now that his eyes filled up his whole face. He still talked about Old Lady Fang and her bad heart, but his barks sounded brittle and he spent more time sleeping or staring quietly into the open.

I was exhausted this morning. Eraser had been

shifting and turning all of last night, whimpering in his sleep. The dustbin Ren had drunk too much and talked loudly until late.

I stayed in the shack trying to get some rest, but finally couldn't ignore the hollow feeling in my stomach any longer. It was time for lunch. The machines would have fallen idle for a little while and Four Fingers Fu and the others would be squatting on the dusty earth slurping up whatever had been dished out to them in little plastic boxes.

It was always difficult to make out exactly what was in their food. But perhaps it was just as well not to know. I stretched slowly, feeling the tightness in my body ease a little and trotted out in search of the dustbin Ren.

It was cold but the sky was bright and my eyes smarted when I looked up. The harsh ratatata of the building machines was in full swing. It must have been earlier than I'd guessed with still a while to go for the noon break.

The air smelt of burning leaves and car smoke. Ren scurried around amongst the machines and the dug up earth wearing hard, yellow hats. His hat was one of Four Fingers Fu's most prized possessions. He kept it cleaner than anything else he had.

He'd put it on top of Eraser's head one evening and laughed as the dog ran around in circles trying to fling it off. 'Get a look at my A-class migrant worker dog, complete with uniform,' he had said while the other dustbin Ren hooted in appreciation.

I was nearing the spot behind the mound of earth that Eraser and I had hidden behind that first day out on this construction site. We no longer felt the need to hide. The Ren who worked here were alright. They left us alone.

I was wondering where Eraser was when almost without knowing why, I felt the hair on the back of my neck tremble. Standing directly in front of me, was a pig-faced Ren, smiling and talking on his mobile phone.

Every instinct in me told me to run and I scrambled behind the pile of earth. My ears felt hot, my tongue dry. I had recognized this Ren, but I didn't know what to do about it. Should I keep hiding or should I show myself? Would he help me or harm me?

In all the many rescue scenarios I had imagined over the days, the one character who had never featured was that rotten egg, Xiao Xu. Yet, there he was, just a few feet away from me. Was I mistaken? Could it really be him? I looked out carefully from behind the mound and there was no doubt. It was Xiao Xu.

I was torn. I'd always had a bad feeling about this Ren. But he was also a link to home. What if he recognized me and took me back to Mr and Mrs A? It could be my only chance. But what was he doing out here in the Stadium? Who was he talking to on his phone?

At first, I strained to catch what he was saying, but

then he began to walk in my direction and his voice carried in the light breeze that had picked up. 'Listen my friend, if you know what's good for you, you'll put your money where Liu Laoban tells you. The man's a genius! Thanks to him, I'm in on the greatest racket in town. It's that cat food, Maomi Deluxe.'

'How does it work? Well, the protein is really the key. What we do is, we mix in some cheap chemical, melamine I think it's called, into the food and here's the beauty, it shows up in tests as protein.'

'Can you believe how cool that is? This melamine stuff is basically some product used in fertilizers. It costs nothing. But we end up with cat food that appears high in protein, that we can charge loads for. It's a beautiful thing, my friend. You really should join us. We'll triple your money in no time.'

'What? The cat model? No, no, he's doing just fine. You don't think we'd let him eat any of the actual product? No way! That would be too risky. What Liu Laoban did was, he just switched the cat food when we filmed the ad. So what was coming out of the Maomi Deluxe box was actually some fancy waiguo product. Imported, top quality. Nothing to worry about on the cat model front, my friend. He's never eaten any real Maomi Deluxe.'

'The other animals? What other animals? Oh, you mean the ones that do end up eating the food? I guess, they'll be fine. These cats are pretty hardy creatures after all. They eat all kinds of junk out of dustbins and what not.'

'And even if a few should die, who would miss them? Good for nothing creatures. They give everyone bing du in any case. We'll all be better off without one or two. Or three!' Xiao Xu snorted loudly.

'Anyway listen, I'm by the Stadium now; just waiting for Liu Laoban. We're going to take a look at the new apartment block we're investing in, right by the Games Village. The units are selling like hot cakes. Unbelievable! These Games are going to be the biggest money-spinner China's ever seen.'

'Of course Liu's got his brocade bag of tricks handy for this project too. The quality inspectors are firmly in our pockets. As for the costs and profits, it's all along Maomi Deluxe lines. Cheap cement and drywall, passed off as top-quality stuff.'

'Look, I've got to go. I'm going across to the apartments now. Liu Laoban will be meeting me there in a few minutes. Let's talk again later, once you've made up your mind if you're in, alright? Take care ge menr!'

Xiao Xu began to walk away and I found myself collapsing in a heap. So many thoughts swirled around in my head. How could Ren be so evil? Was Soyabean safe? What if Liu Laoban had forgotten to switch the food he ate, even once? He would be sick. In real danger.

I had to find a way of getting back home. It was no longer just about me and Eraser. I had to get back to warn Soyabean; to find a way of warning Mrs A.

There were Ren out there feeding their pets this poisoned food. Cats could be dying as a result. I had to find a way to stop it.

But I wasn't a very big cat or even a particularly brave one. And I was lost. How in the World was I going to expose Xiao Xu and his friend?

I felt ill with worry and hatred. That terrible, terrible Xiao Xu. He'd pretended to be Soyabean's friend and everyone had fallen for it.

I felt a damp nose on my side. It was Eraser. 'Where've you been Tofu?' he yapped. 'I haven't seen you all morning. It's lunch time. Let's go find Four Fingers Fu. I'm starving.'

It was only then that I noticed that the machines had fallen silent. Because in my head it felt like a thousand voices were shouting. I decided not to say anything to the dog. Eraser was miserable enough already and I wasn't sure he could handle any more bad news. All this protein stuff would be too complicated to explain to him in any case. He was sweet but not too bright.

I followed Eraser to where the dustbin Ren were eating lunch, in a daze. There was a hard knot in my belly.

Four Fingers Fu noticed something was up. 'Oi! Comrade cat, what's got into you today?' he said ruffling my fur, when I turned my face away from the food he held out for me. 'Not hungry? Still full from all that goose liver and pig's trotters last night eh?' he joked.

Then his eyes turned concerned and he scratched me under the chin. 'Maomi, you have to eat. Must keep your spirits up now. Come on take a bite,' he urged.

'Leave that dratted cat alone. If she don't want it, give it to me,' interrupted Old Zhu who was sitting next to him. He snatched the morsel of food Four Fingers Fu was holding out with his chopsticks and stuck it in his mouth, swallowing without chewing. His breath reeked of alcohol even though it was the middle of the day.

A loud clanging broke out. It was the construction site supervisor signalling the end of the lunch break. I noticed Four Fingers Fu turning back to look at me for a moment before he disappeared into the construction pit. He was a very kind Ren. But it was Xiao Xu I had on my mind. The very worst sort of Ren there was.

That night was possibly the longest of my life. The cigarette smoke hung heavy in the cramped hut and the dustbin Ren, playing their endless games of cards, took on a nightmarish quality. I felt trapped and helpless, lying there in a corner of the phlegm-spotted floor.

For the first time I allowed myself to wonder what would happen if Da Ge didn't find me. Would I spend the rest of my life here with Eraser and Four Fingers Fu? What about after the Birds Nest Stadium had been built? And what about Soyabean? What if he had somehow ended up eating the real Maomi Deluxe?

The moment the sky lightened I snuck out of the shack. I hadn't got any sleep but I couldn't stand being stuck inside the tiny space any longer. Eraser was still inside, snoring. He could sleep through anything, that dog. A bit like Soyabean.

There were a few planks of wood strewn around outside; useful for a good scratch. My nails were horribly long. I stretched out my front paws and was about to start scraping away when a movement to the right caught my eye.

I swung around to look. The largest, most orange cat I'd ever seen was sitting a few steps away staring at me, unblinkingly, curiously. His fur was matted and large cuts marked his face and ears but there was something magnificent about him. He reminded me very much of someone.

We stared at each other. And then he spoke. 'We've been looking everywhere for you, kid.' Instantly I knew exactly who it was: Soyabean's Ba. I tried to speak but I was so stunned, my voice disappeared.

The orange cat smiled, it was a sideway, rakish grin. 'What's the matter? Cat got your tongue?'

'Ba?' I finally managed to gasp. 'Are you Soyabean's Ba?' 'In the flesh, kid,' he replied and I felt tears well up in my eyes. His voice was just like Soyabean's, only deeper.

'Tofu?' Eraser's tiny bark inquired. 'Tofu, who is

this? What's going on?' The dog had woken up and come out. Sleep still hung on his breath. He looked confused, guarded.

'Strange friends you've got,' drawled Ba, looking Eraser over. 'It's what threw my Ghost Street Gang boys. We'd sent out a description of a tawny girl cat on her own. Didn't expect you to have company,' Ba paused, and raised an ear, 'of the canine variety.'

'Who is this Tofu?' Eraser asked again, shrilly. 'Do you know him?' I turned towards the dog and put my nose on his. 'Eraser, didn't I always tell you it was only a matter of time? Well, the time has come xiao pengyou, little friend. We've been found.'

'Wasn't easy, mind you,' interrupted Ba. 'Most of the cat gangs from this area have been driven out, what with all this construction and noise. It's no longer a suitable residence, wouldn't you agree? So our resources were spread quite thinly on the ground around here.'

'But there's this one young fellow. Wasn't too sure about him to start with; he's the white fur, blue eyes type. Not usually the quickest of cats. But this lad's turned out to be quite promising; might even be worth having him join my boys in Ghost Street.'

'His mum was in one of the gangs that used to frequent this area, before all the old residents were cleared off to make space for this Stadium thingummyjig. And so he knew the lay of the land, so as to speak. He's been staking it out for a few weeks now. Took him a while to get the message across to us about having potentially spotted the target—that's you, hanging around with some migrant worker Ren, but he got it through in the end.'

'And so here I am. Very pleased the tip-off came good and very pleased to make your acquaintance finally, kid. I believe my son, Soyabean, I think he's called these days, has lost a bit of weight worrying about you. Not that that's a bad thing by all reports, mind you!'

'Well, we best be taking you home, hadn't we? Although, I'm afraid I won't have the pleasure of escorting you back myself; got things to do. Busy, busy, busy. That's me! But give my boy a rub on the nose from me when you see him.'

'Wait. Wait!' I meowed, urgently. 'Soyabean's Ba, don't leave us. Where are you going? Who's going to take us home?' But Ba was already loping off into the distance in a blur of orange.

'Number Three, Number Three, don't worry. Did you think your Da Ger wouldn't come to take you home?'

I began to tremble. I had imagined this voice and these words so many times I couldn't be sure I wasn't just dreaming it all again. I turned around carefully, slowly. Could it really be?

'Hello, baby sister. You've been leading us on a merry chase,' grinned my brother, flashing the many gaps in his teeth. His right eye was blackened and a swarm of what looked liked ticks hung off his ears but to me he was absolutely beautiful; a dashing hero.

In a second I was on his paws, feeling his rough tongue lick my tears away. 'You'll be fine now, Number Three. It's all over. I've found you, just like I promised,' Da Ge murmured over and over again.

Eraser began to yap in excitement and I had to disentangle myself from my brother to introduce them. Da Ge tried to keep his distance from the dog although he managed to mutter a polite, 'Any friend of my sister's a friend of mine.' But Eraser kept leaping up to him jabbering away hysterically.

'Will you take us back to our Hutong, Da Ge? Old Lady Fang will be so pleased to see me again. She must have been very sad these past weeks. I can't believe you're actually here. Tofu told me you would come. She told me everyday. But I had begun to think that maybe she was wrong.'

'Look dog, not so close. Can you sit still for a minute?' asked Da Ge backing away from Eraser as he jumped up and down. I swatted the dog over his ears and gave him a warning look. He finally calmed down, all though his smile remained so wide, drool dripped through it.

I could finally get a word in edgeways. I had to ask the question that had been weighing on me. 'Da Ge, how is Soyabean? Is he well? He hasn't been sick has he?

'Soyabean? He's just fine. Our boys keep a regular

eye on him and there's not much to report. Been moping about a bit, understandably, but he's in better shape than you for one. Gone a bit skinny you have, kid. Still, nothing a few days of rest and hot food won't fix.'

'I'll tell you what, though, there is some good news. No more white vans will be coming after you. The bing du virus is finally dying down.' Da Ge cocked his head to one side and paused for a second to give his ear a vigorous scratch before continuing.

'Ren are calming down. There've been no new attacks on animals for a while now and they've stopped wearing those God-awful face masks. We're all feeling a lot safer, I can tell you. Got a bit hairy out there for a while, but it's passing.'

'There is something else a bit strange though, Number Three. Ren might be out of the woods with that blasted virus, but it seems there's some new kind of cat bing du going around. We've been getting word on the street of dozens of cats falling sick, some even dying. Odd thing is it affects only pets. Us alley cats are doing fine.'

I felt cold all over. It was true then what I'd heard Xiao Xu saying on the phone. Cats were eating poisoned Maomi Deluxe and falling ill. 'It's not bing du, Da Ge,' I said to my brother grimly. 'It's Maomi Deluxe, the cat food that Soyabean was modelling for.'

'What?' asked Da Ge, his mouth hanging open with surprise. 'What are you talking about? You better explain that kid.'

chapter eleven

SOYABEAN

Frustration

She was back! It was the most wonderful thing. I felt like running around the courtyard meowing at the top of my voice. In fact, it's what I was doing when Auntie Li came at me with her broom. But she was really happy too, even though she tried to hide it. 'So much fuss over a cat,' she muttered but I saw that she was smiling.

It had all begun with a scratching on the door. I was in the yard when I heard it. At first I thought it was one of the young Ren from the hutong. They fooled around under the big tree outside the siheyuan doors when they returned from school in the afternoon.

But there was something about the scratching. It was a cat-like scrabbling; furtive, persistent. It was, in fact, a very Tofu-cat-like scratching. Barely had that thought crossed my mind that Mrs A had come out of the study, her eyes staring wildly.

'What was that?' she'd asked although there was no one but me in the yard. The scratching continued.

'Did you hear that?' she'd asked again and begun to run towards the tall, red doors. She'd flung them open and there had been Tofu; thinner and dirtier than before, but unmistakably Tofu.

I'd flown towards them, hurtling across the yard faster than I had ever imagined I could, but even then I was too late. Mrs A had scooped up Tofu in her arms and hurried away towards the main pavilion.

I'd tried to follow, but the door to the living room swung shut just as I'd been about to go through. Through the netted window screens, I'd seen Mrs A examine every part of Tofu. 'Oh Baby Cat!' she'd kept exclaiming over and over again.

That's when I'd begun to dash about the courtyard until Auntie Li came to shush me. In the end, I returned to the window sill and waited, impatiently, for Mrs A finally to notice me, my face scrunched up against the screen.

'Soyabean, come on in,' she laughed lightly, happily, holding the door open for me. 'Your friend is back. It's a miracle, but Tofu's here.' She bent down to ruffle my fur. 'Go say hello to her. I'm going to make a few calls.'

She hurried off towards the study and then it was just Tofu and me in the room all alone. Tofu had always been a small cat but sitting up on the big sofa Mrs A had placed her on, she looked really tiny and frail. This was the moment I had been dreaming of for days. But now that it was here I felt at a loss; almost a little shy. It was a most unusual feeling for me. I was quite a daring cat by most standards. Even the biggest rat didn't scare me.

But of course, a lot had changed these last few weeks. I had so much to be ashamed of: the fool I'd made of myself over the modelling business; the terrible way I'd let down Tofu. It had all taken its toll on my confidence.

What could I say to her for her to forgive me? How could I make her understand how sorry I was? I didn't know if I could find the right meows.

I stared miserably at the floor and in the end it was Tofu who spoke first. She leapt off the sofa and padded up to me, touching her nose to mine. It felt cold on the outside but on the inside I felt warmer than I had in a longer time.

'Soyabean,' she whispered. 'Thank God you're alright. I've been very worried about you.'

What an odd, most wonderful cat Tofu was. She'd been lost and alone all this time and she was worried about me!

'I'm so, so sorry Tofu. I was a very bad cat. I should have been watching out for you instead of looking at the Maomi Deluxe ad. And you were right about Xiao Xu and Liu Laoban and everything. There's something wrong with Maomi Deluxe and Madam Wang says cats are getting ill. And I just don't know what to do. I've missed you so much and I'm so happy you're back!'

The words came pouring out in a storm, now that my tongue had loosened. I just kept blabbering until I ran out of breath. We spent the rest of the afternoon scrunched up together on the sofa and Tofu told me everything: about the white van and the Ren with long fingernails who had kidnapped her; about her escape with Eraser later that night; and about life with dustbin Ren by the Stadium.

I couldn't help but feel a twinge of jealousy. I was the one who had always been the brave cat, the big cat, the cat who wanted to explore the World and yet Tofu knew so much more of it now. It was difficult to get my head around.

She'd been my little sidekick since we were kittens. It was strange to imagine her being so bold and having all these adventures and that too with a dog! Eraser. Bit of a silly name, I thought.

Tofu insisted that this dog was a good sort but I must say, I had my reservations. It just wasn't natural for a cat and dog to be so friendly. But, I kept my thoughts to myself. I'd been wrong before and Tofu was wiser than I'd supposed. If she said Eraser was alright, perhaps he was, however unbelievable it sounded.

All the action with Four Fingers Fu and Lao Li and Old Zhu sounded quite exciting too. Of course most cats might have found it frightening but I wasn't easily scared. The food didn't sound too great, though. I guess it was just as well I hadn't had to eat it. But the Stadium! It must have been unbearably wonderful to see it being built.

My life was so dull in comparison. I'd never been kidnapped. I'd never escaped. I had starred in an ad but what a disaster that had turned out to be. It seemed unfair that I'd mostly just been cooped up at home feeling miserable while Tofu had been out there in the thick of it.

I knew I shouldn't have felt like that. Tofu was a generous cat. She hadn't scolded me at all. She'd forgiven me before I'd even asked her to. But that was a bit annoying as well. She was such a good cat. It made me feel guiltier and guiltier.

Every prick of annoyance disappeared, however, once Tofu began to tell me about Xiao Xu. I was shocked at the story. My tail went rigid; the hair along my back bristled.

Now, I finally understood what Liu Laoban had meant about the protein. It was even worse than I'd imagined. What a heartless, wicked Ren Xiao Xu was. I thought of Nai Nai and how sad she would be if she knew what her grandson was doing. And of how betrayed Mr and Mrs A would feel if they understood how Xiao Xu had used them for his wicked schemes.

But most of all I felt frustrated. More and more Ren were out there buying poisoned Maomi Deluxe and feeding it to their cats, after watching my ad. Everyone thought I was a hero; a celebrity. But what no one knew was that I was also a murderer. I felt hot, feverish. Cats were dying and I couldn't think how to stop it.

'We have to find a way to warn everyone,' meowed Tofu anxiously. 'It's got to be us. Da Ge said so too.'

'What do you mean? What did he say?' I asked.

'Well, when I told him what's going on with Xiao Xu and Maomi Deluxe he became very worried, of course. But the more he thought about it the more he realized there was little he or your Ba could do to help.'

'You see, it's only Ren who can expose Xiao Xu and put an end to the whole racket. But dustbin cats must stay away from Ren. It's us pets who have access to them. So it's up to us to fix this mess somehow, Soyabean.'

Her eyes were getting larger as she spoke. Her voice shook with urgency. 'I would do it if I could, but I'm no good at communicating with Ren. You know that. You're the one who can always make yourself understood. Can't you think of some way of warning Mrs A?' she meowed.

'Oh Tofu! How can I? I don't really speak Ren language. I know I can be quite good at getting Mrs A to understand some things but this is just so complicated. Pointing a paw at a box of Maomi Deluxe won't do the trick, will it? She'll probably just think I'm hungry or something.'

I felt so powerless it made me mad. I swallowed hard before going on. 'You don't know this but I bit Xiao Xu the last time he was here after I'd realized he was plotting something suspicious with Liu Laoban. Mrs A didn't understand at all. She only got upset with me.'

I thumped my tail down in despair. 'I know you're used to me having all the answers Tofu, but the fact is I'm at my wit's end. Of course we've got to do something, but I can't figure out what.'

Tofu opened her mouth to meow in reply but before we could discuss it any further the door to the living room opened and Mr A came bursting in. 'There you are you little thing,' he said rushing up to Tofu. 'What a scare you gave us all. Where have you been? How did you find your way back?'

'It's because she's a very clever cat and a brave cat. Isn't that right?' Mrs A, who had come in behind her husband, crooned. 'Well,' said Mr A sitting down with Tofu on his lap. 'I don't suppose we'll ever know for sure. She must have gotten away from that van like Madam Wang told you. And somehow she managed to come back.'

He looked thoughtful, but continued to stroke Tofu's back. 'It's a miracle really,' Mrs A smiled.

The days that followed were difficult. It was

wonderful to have Tofu home but at the same time I was awfully frustrated. On the surface everything was back to normal.

Auntie Li started the day by making us extra-special breakfasts. Well, the breakfasts were really for Tofu because she had become skinny and needed fattening up, but her tummy was too small to eat much. It was only natural that I got her leftovers. It's no good to waste food after all.

The mornings were really icy now and I spent a lot of time indoors, lounging around on the sofa, coming up with impractical plans to expose Xiao Xu. Tofu remained outside, high in the leafless pomegranate tree, staring into the sky. Sometimes the air was so cold it bit through the fur, but that didn't stop her.

I tried asking her why she liked being in the tree so much. She never answered the question. 'It must be so cold in Four Fingers Fu's shack now,' she would say instead, that typically dreamy Tofu look in her eyes. 'Dustbin Ren don't have heating like we do in the siheyuan.' I would eventually give up trying to get a decent answer out of her and go back to the warm living room.

I knew Tofu felt bad about having left the dustbin Ren so abruptly without saying bye. Da Ge had insisted on their leaving the Stadium construction site immediately. It was a long trip home and he had wanted them to make it back before it became dark.

Tofu never told me much about that journey. All

she said was that the World was very loud. I knew she was sad for Four Fingers Fu because he was poor. She felt too much pain, that cat. She even missed the dog, Eraser.

At least he was safely home with Old Lady Fang from the corner shop. We got regular news of him from Auntie Li who went to the shop most days to buy fruit or fresh yoghurt. Yoghurt was one of my favourite foods and I would swish my tail while I waited by the main door for Auntie to come back home with it.

'Ai! You fat cat, always hungry,' she would grumble when she saw me waiting. I wasn't put off by her calling me fat because I knew that it was a fact that I was rather good looking. 'Fat' was more a term of endearment, I think.

And she always scooped out a spoon of the yoghurt for me later.

It was after one of her trips to the shop that I heard Auntie Li telling Mrs A about Old Lady Fang being so grateful Eraser had returned that she had gone to the Lama Temple and spent a whole lot of money burning incense sticks in thanks.

I didn't quite understand why anyone would burn funny-smelling sticks just because their dog had come home. Ren could be inexplicable. I wasn't too sure I'd be particularly happy to see a dog at all, let alone go and thank someone for it. Of course I didn't mention this to Tofu. She was quite sensitive about Eraser.

Things really did seem to be getting back to usual. Now that the bing du virus was under control, the neighbours had started to come around again.

Xiao Wang stopped by several times. Mrs A always looked a bit nervous when she found him at the door. I supposed it was because she suspected he might have brought more crickets for me. But he never did.

I felt a little disappointed, naturally, but didn't have much time to fret about it, being too busy trying to figure out a plan to expose the Maomi Deluxe fraud. Neither Tofu nor I had had much luck thinking up anything. Matters were coming to a crisis point, however.

Yesterday Mrs A, Tofu and I were warming ourselves by the radiator in the kitchen when Xiao Wang dropped by. Auntie Li came in to tell us he had come.

'What, not again?' said Mrs A sounding a little impatient. 'He's a sweet boy but sometimes I think he comes around only to use the toilet,' she grumbled.

I hadn't thought about that. But it was true. Xiao Wang did always ask to use the loo when he visited. I suppose it was because the public toilet outside had still not been renovated.

I felt a twinge of responsibility. The hutong Ren had been so excited when I had become a celebrity model. They had expected the government would transform the neighbourhood now that a star was living in it. Frankly, so had I.

This government that everyone was always going on about didn't sound very impressive to me.

My thoughts were interrupted by Auntie Li ushering in Xiao Wang to the kitchen. He took off his gloves and blew on his hands. 'Good afternoon, Tai Tai,' he said. 'I hope you don't mind me dropping in.'

'Not at all,' said Mrs A politely. 'Come in and sit with me and the cats. Would you like some tea?' She paused for a moment. 'Unless you would like to use the toilet first?'

'Thank you so much Tai Tai,' Xiao Wang replied grinning. 'I will use it, but later if you don't mind. First let me say hello to Soyabean.'

Tofu had already slunk away under the side table by now. She still didn't like being around Ren. Strange, considering how she seemed to have managed fine with the dustbin Ren. Xiao Wang bent down to scratch my neck and I began to purr. But then he broke the awful news.

'Tai Tai,' he said looking up at Mrs A. 'I have something exciting to tell you. My Ma has finally agreed to get me a cat of my own. I've told her it's got to look just like Soyabean and of course we will be feeding it Maomi Deluxe.'

I froze mid-purr. My blood turned to ice.

'Maomi Deluxe?' Mrs A replied. 'That's expensive stuff, Xiao Wang. I would just give your cat bits of whatever you cook at home. That's what we do with Soyabean and Tofu. Come to think of it, I don't think we've ever actually bought any Maomi Deluxe for them.'

Xiao Wang's face took on a stubborn look. 'But, Maomi Deluxe is the best food out there for cats, Tai Tai. Everyone knows that. It's high in protein you see.' He stood up stiffly. 'And we might be poor but that doesn't mean we won't treat our cat right.'

Mrs A shrugged. 'Of course Xiao Wang, I didn't mean to imply anything. Your cat will be a lucky one to have such a good family to look after him.' Xiao Wang and Mrs A continued to chat for a while but I couldn't pay any attention to what they were saying. There was a loud buzzing noise in my ears.

Later, when Xiao Wang finally left, Tofu came crawling out from under the table. We looked at each other silently, frantically. What were we going to do?

Auntie Li was pottering around the kitchen, clearing away the tea cups. 'Everyone has gone cat mad,' she said to Mrs A wiping clean the table. 'Xiao Wang's family is poor. They can ill afford to send him to school and now they're going to get a pet and feed it Maomi Deluxe of all fancy foods! Heavens! Even that Fat Tao is wandering around claiming he's going to get a pet.'

'Fat Tao?' said Mrs A sharply. 'But doesn't he hate animals?' 'Who knows Tai Tai?' answered Auntie Li, fingering a stray lock of her grey hair back into place. 'I think it's all just a ploy to make sure he doesn't get into trouble over all that anti-cat and dog nonsense he was full of during the bing du scare. Now that it's over he's worried he might be accused of being part of those kidnapping mobs.'

She snorted. 'He's walking around with a slimy grin plastered all over his face saying how much he loves cats and how he's looking to take one in as a pet! I wouldn't trust him for a second. Ivory tusks don't suddenly sprout from a dog's mouth, do they?'

Tofu and I spent all of last night bundled up together, racking our brains for a plan. Biting Xiao Xu again if I got a chance wouldn't work. Pointing at a box of Maomi Deluxe and meowing loudly was out as well. Could we somehow get Madam Wang to pursue her suspicions further?

That sounded promising but we couldn't figure out how. We were locked up all day in the siheyuan and couldn't get to Madam Wang if we wanted to. And even if we could how would we make her understand what was going on? It seemed totally impossible.

In the end we gave up and tried to get some sleep, or at least I did. Tofu went out and climbed up the tree again. She said it helped her think.

That morning I made my way to the As' bedroom after breakfast. I'd decided to treat myself with a nap on their soft bed. I thought a good snooze might help my tired brain work better. The silk sheets were delicious. After only a few minutes I was about to float off to sleep when the telephone began ringing.

I heard Mrs A pick it up in the next room. She talked for quite a long time but I couldn't catch what she was saying. And I was too drowsy to try very hard. I must have dozed off because I got quite a start when Mrs A banged open the doors to the bedroom.

I looked up sleepily. Mrs A's face was flushed. 'Oh Soyabean, I have some wonderful news for you,' she said breathlessly. I cocked my ears. What ever could it be?

'That was Xiao Xu on the phone,' she said. I felt alarm bells clanging in my chest. 'You know there have been times I haven't quite approved of that young man, but he was really very nice just now,' she continued.

'I thought maybe he was calling to kick up a fuss about your having bitten him. After all people can sue over those kinds of things. But he doesn't seem to hold a grudge at all. He hardly mentioned the bite.'

Mrs A knelt down in front of me and gave me a quick massage. 'You're such a beautiful cat Soyabean, I'm not at all surprised, but the big news is that your Maomi Deluxe ad has just won an award for TV commercial of the year.'

I stared at her blankly but she kept babbling enthusiastically. 'Can you imagine? The National Advertising Council of China has selected your ad, out of hundreds! Xiao Xu said they made special mention of a certain cat model and his realistic acting skills. Can you guess who?'

Of course I could.

'It's you Soyabean!' she went on her voice squeaky with excitement. The higher her voice rose, the lower my heart sank.

'And you'll never believe what else!' she went on. Was there to be no end to this nightmare?

'There's going to be a big televised award ceremony in a few days time and you've been invited to star in it.' Mrs A glowed as she spoke.

'The organizers want to do a live re-enactment of the winning ad in front of a huge studio audience. It will be beamed across China on CCTV-1, the national channel. Can you imagine?' Mrs A picked me up and gave me a tight squeeze. 'I'm very proud of you Soyabean. You are a star!' she said kissing me on the nose.

chapter twelve

TOFU

The Award

The sky was bubbling over. I had been perched in the pomegranate tree watching the clouds gather and dance all morning, trying to still my nerves. The leafless branches were like thorns jabbing at me when I'd made my way up. But I had welcomed the hurt. It had given me something to focus on other than the thudding in my chest.

It could all go wrong so easily. We'd talked over the plan for days. But it was the kind of plan that needed luck and no amount of talking could guarantee that.

When Soyabean had come panting to tell me about the TV commercial award Maomi Deluxe was going to get, the idea burst through me, like an over-filled balloon. I hadn't even consciously thought it out. It was as if it had been sitting inside my head, fully formed, just waiting for the right trigger to float up and away.

Soyabean could be such a courageous cat. He'd agreed to the plan immediately, without pausing to ponder the consequences were anything to go awry. In fact he'd seemed excited. I guess the prospect of actually doing something rather than moping around in frustration, like we had been for so long, was exciting.

But I was grateful it wasn't me who would have to be up there facing a live audience of unknown Ren on national TV. My tummy flip-flopped just imagining it. Thankfully, Soyabean was a more confident cat.

But I was worried about him. What if some real, poisoned Maomi Deluxe made it to his bowl this time? What if things went according to plan but the Ren in the audience still didn't cotton on? There were so many unknowns. And what were we but two cats in a World of Ren. Could our plan really work?

Of course we weren't totally alone. We'd talked everything over with Da Ge as well. He'd been coming by most nights when the roof was filled with shadows and no one noticed an extra, cat-shaped one.

At first he'd been skeptical. I wasn't surprised. It wasn't a fool proof plan. But as he ended up agreeing, at least it was a plan. The award ceremony could be our only chance. We had to give it a shot. The price of not acting was simply too high.

I heard a whiny meowing at the bottom of the tree. It was Soyabean. I clambered down, wincing as the branches scratched at me. 'What are you doing up there again, today of all days,' he said crossly, even before I had made it to the foot. I wasn't quite sure why but Soyabean seemed to find it really annoying when I spent time in the tree. I knew he preferred being indoors but it wasn't like I forced him to come out with me.

I thought it may have had something to do with him being a tom cat. They could be so restless; impatient. But I suppose any cat could be forgiven for being a bit agitated under the circumstances.

Soyabean must have been nervous, not that he would admit it. Tom cats!

'Is it time?' I asked him. His eyes were shadowed with anxiety. 'Yes. He should be here any moment.'

Xiao Xu was going to pick up Soyabean to take him to the CCTV auditorium. The show wasn't until later in the afternoon but Xiao Xu had said it was a long drive.

'Oh Tofu!' Soyabean meowed. He sounded squeaky. 'I don't know if I'll be able to control myself. How am I going to sit with that monster in a car for who knows how long pretending that everything is okay when all I'll really want to do is scratch him so hard he won't be able to stop crying for a week; or perhaps a month; or maybe . . .'

Soyabean looked thoughtful. 'Do you think it's

possible to make someone cry for a year? Or is that too long?'

'Soyabean,' I said as sternly as I could. 'You've got to stop thinking foolish thoughts. Pull yourself together!' He looked peeved.

'It's all very well for you to say. You're not the one who's going to be out there. You'll just be sitting right here on a soft watching it all on TV.' I took a deep breath. Tom cats could be terribly childish.

'Listen Soyabean,' I said, more gently this time. 'Remember what a great actor you are. You're even receiving an award for your acting. You can pull it off. It'll be challenging, but we're all depending on you. I believe in you.'

Soyabean's chest puffed out and the look in his eyes softened. 'I know you're counting on me, Tofu. I'm sorry. All this responsibility can just be a bit too much sometimes. But don't worry. I really am a very good actor.'

We smiled at each other; cat smiles, not with our lips but our ears. There was a sharp rapping on the door. Xiao Xu!

'You okay,' I asked? 'Sure,' Soyabean replied, cockily. There was a wink in his meow.

Mr A came out of the study and opened the front doors. 'Ni Hao!' said Xiao Xu, stepping in from the outside, baring his yellowed teeth. I thought back to how happily he'd boasted to his friend about adding that poison melamine to Maomi Deluxe. There had been no guilt in his voice at all, only greed. A Ren who could poison cats without a care was truly a Ren with a poisoned heart himself.

'Ni hao! Ni hao Xiao Xu,' replied Mr A shaking hands with him. 'Huan Ying. Welcome!' Mr A turned around to call out for Soyabean.

'Where's the famous star?' he said looking about the yard, until he caught sight of us scrunched up by the tree. 'There you are Soyabean! Come here and say ni hao.'

He turned back to face Xiao Xu. 'We've been so excited since you called with the news. It was totally unexpected. But we're really proud of our Soyabean. Thank you for making all of this possible.'

My claws came unsheathed. I wasn't a very aggressive cat but hearing Mr A actually thank that devil Xiao Xu made me want to scratch him as hard as Soyabean had been talking about; enough to make him cry for a year, at least.

'No need to thank me,' Xiao Xu replied sanctimoniously. 'My Nai Nai always taught me that anything can be accomplished with hard work and ambition.' I could see he was trying to look modest, but a sneer lurked in his voice.

'It's you waiguo ren I should be thanking for fattening up the maomi so well on all the expensive treats you give him,' he continued. 'That's very kind of you Xiao Xu,' replied Mr A. 'I'm sorry my wife isn't here to say hello. She's getting her hair done for the big occasion. We'll be driving down later as discussed. Thanks again for organizing passes for us to attend the show.'

'Mei Shir. No problem. It's going to be a big crowd. We should be able to triple sales of Maomi Deluxe after today,' Xiao Xu chuckled. He glanced at his wrist watch.

'It's time we were going. Liu Laoban wants to go through a dress rehearsal to make sure we're ready for the live show.' He looked across to Soyabean and me and clicked his fingers. It was a malignant sound. 'Come along now Maomi. Come to Xiao Xu.'

Soyabean quickly flicked his whiskers on mine in farewell. He turned and began to walk towards Xiao Xu. There was a spring in his step but I couldn't help feel he was a lamb-like cat being led to slaughter. 'Be careful. Xiao xin,' I whispered.

When the front door closed after them, I felt like I had been slapped in the face, hard. All the wind left my body.

The next few hours crawled by. I was hoping Da Ge might show up so we could reconfirm the arrangements one last time but the rooftop remained empty. Mrs A returned from the hairdressers looking very pretty. She'd had her hair swept up in a bun and was wearing a Chinese style qipao dress.

Time hung emptily. Finally Mr and Mrs A were ready to leave. Mrs A kissed me bye on the nose; Mr A tutted disapprovingly. And then they were off in a swirl of perfume and excitement, chattering away excitedly.

'Well Tofu,' said Auntie Li as the doors slammed shut. 'It's going to be you, me and the TV this afternoon.' She bent down and gave my ears a quick, absent-minded scratch before pottering off towards the kitchen.

When she emerged a few minutes later she was carrying a pot of hot, fragrant tea. 'Come along then,' she said. 'Let's make ourselves comfortable on the sofa.' We padded into the living room together and sat down. Auntie Li switched on the TV with the remote control.

A huge room full of Ren filled the screen. At the far end was an elevated stage decked out with a red banner. Big white characters were painted onto it. 'The National Advertising Council of China, Commercial of the Year Award,' it read.

'There is already a buzz of anticipation here in the CCTV studio.' The camera cut to a very thin, female Ren dressed in a glittering white qipao dress. 'We will be bringing you every minute of the glamour, the excitement, the stars and the gossip,' she said breathlessly.

'Hmph,' muttered Auntie Li next to me, putting on her glasses. 'I didn't want to say anything to Mrs A but that Xiao Xu could have got a pass for me as well now, couldn't he?'

'Probably didn't fancy inviting a migrant worker. It

wouldn't do to have a real person amongst all this glamour, I suppose.' Auntie Li snorted and then put her hand on my head. 'Never mind Tofu. Cats and migrant workers might not be invited but we're probably better off watching it all here from this nice sofa anyway.'

Cats not invited? Well, Auntie Li might be in for a surprise, I thought. My blood was racing, my head spinning. There was no going back now.

'Amongst the studio audience tonight we have some of the biggest names from show biz: Wang Bing, Li Na and Ting Ting,' continued the announcer. The camera zoomed into the faces of several Ren in succession.

I had never seen any of them before but they must have been famous because the audience clapped loudly for each of them. I thought their skin looked unnaturally tight. They all had very nice white teeth though; so different from the chipped, stained mouths of dustbin Ren.

Soyabean had taught me a lot of special TV commercial words. They mostly had to do with camera angles: zoom, pan, long-shot, close up. Soyabean said a long-shot in profile was his most flattering angle. He thought it made him look slimmer. I thought he should simply eat less if he wanted to look slimmer but I knew better than to tell him that.

The camera panned around the room and I felt a little ping of excitement. I had recognized a face. It was Madam Wang. Her upright figure was unmistakable. She sat clutching a pen and piece of paper, the grim expression on her face very different from the vacant, smiling faces of the other Ren around her.

Auntie Li noticed her as well. 'Isn't that Madam Wang or whatever her name is,' she asked peering intently through her glasses. 'Uff! I'm probably the only one in the whole city not invited,' she grumbled taking a long slurp of tea.

My eyes were glued to the screen. Madam Wang being in the audience was an unexpected piece of luck. Of all the Ren in the World, she was the one who had the best chance of understanding our plan.

Then my heart gave another leap. Madam Wang had turned to talk to the Ren sitting on her right. At first I didn't recognize the man. It was a long-shot and I couldn't see very clearly. But as the camera zoomed in closer, the gentle quietness of his face was unmistakable. My eyes began to fill with tears but I brushed them aside impatiently. I wanted to feast on this face uninterrupted. After all, I had held it in my heart for so many months. It was Old Man Zhao, the first Ren I had ever known and also one of the best Ren I had ever known.

He looked older than I remembered; more creased, more grey. But there was kindness in the curve of his mouth and in the depths of his eyes. The same kindness I had glimpsed when he shared scraps of liver with Mama or put out a bowl of milk for my brothers and me.

Madam Wang whispered something in his ear. I would have given my tail to know what it was but all I could hear was the TV presenter's twittering. 'The moment we have all been waiting for is almost here,' she announced.

The camera panned the room again. Everyone wore an earnest, expectant look. 'There they are! Look Tofu, its Tai Tai!' Auntie Li was bouncing up and down on the sofa pointing her finger at Mr and Mrs A. They were sitting up front by the stage and besides them was Soyabean's Nai Nai.

She was beaming brightly at Mrs A who was holding her hand. I guessed they must have been discussing Soyabean's great achievement, what a fine actor he was and so on. Well, his most important acting role was only a few moments away as the announcer Ren kept reminding everyone.

'Ladies, Gentlemen, Friends,' a new Ren had joined the breathless, thin one on the stage. He was tall and broad shouldered, dressed in a dark, shiny suit. 'Please give a warm round of applause for Mr Ma Jun, esteemed President of the National Advertising Council of China.' The room filled with noisy clapping. I could see Mr and Mrs A joining in enthusiastically.

A short, podgy Ren made his way onto the stage. His belly jiggled loosely as he climbed up the steps. He held out the palms of his hands and waved them up and down. The clapping began to quieten.

'Ladies, Gentlemen, Friends, Comrades. Dajia Hao. Hello everyone.' The Ren in the studio fell silent. Back in the siheyuan living room Auntie Li had gone quiet too. 'It may be cold outside on this autumn day,' the fat Ren continued, 'but I feel warm in my heart on this very special occasion.'

Another round of applause burst out. The Ren waved his hands up and down once again. When it was calmer, he continued.

'The China National Advertising Award is one of the world's toughest advertising competitions, representing the true spirit of Chinese creative excellence. In presenting it we are proud to honour a company that is not only inventive but also brings about a real contribution to society and consumers.'

'Maomi Deluxe is just such a company and we are happy to have its CEO Mr Liu Libo with us today.' The camera swung around to the front row of the audience where Liu Laoban sat smirking with Xiao Xu right next to him. It was odd to hear Liu Laoban being referred to by his proper name: Liu Libo.

But if our plan worked, that was a name we would all hear a lot more often.

'Mr Liu has brought to the Chinese pet lover the kind of high-quality cat food that was until now only available abroad. Through his efforts Chinese pet owners can proudly buy premium Chinese cat food rather than waste their hard earned money on foreign brands.'

'He has of course also brought to the people of China a character that has worked his way into all of our hearts; one of the best loved figures on TV today: Soyabean the cat!' More thunderous applause followed. Even Auntie Li broke out clapping, her unhappiness at not being invited to the show temporarily forgotten.

The fat President continued his speech. 'We are now pleased to present to all of you here in the studio as well as all those watching on their TV sets back home, a live performance of your favourite advertisement starring none other than the adorably fluffy Soyabean himself.'

The lights went dim for a few seconds and when the screen brightened, the scene on the stage had changed.

Another man, whom I recognized as the actor from the Maomi Deluxe ad, was pottering around what looked like a kitchen. And right in the centre of the stage, glowing golden under a spotlight sat Soyabean.

I could hardly bear to watch, I was so nervous, but I forced my eyes to remain open. Soyabean looked composed. There wasn't even a hint of what was to follow in his behaviour.

'Time for dinner maomi,' the Ren on stage trilled out walking towards Soyabean with a bowl. He put it down and filled it with food taken out of a packet with waiguo writing on it. I had seen this same scene

on TV so many times. But this time things were going to be different. Or were they? Would Soyabean keep his nerve?

On the screen Soyabean sniffed suspiciously at the bowl and then turned his face away, sulking. There were a few titters from the audience. I had to admit Soyabean really was a good actor.

At this point a female Ren walked in, the Tai Tai of the house. She looked at her husband, Soyabean and the bowl of untouched cat food between them and shook her head. 'Old Lu,' she said, 'when you come home in the evening would you rather have a steaming plate of fried pork noodles or a cold, crusty sandwich?'

'Noodles,' replied the man without a pause.

'Of course you would, because Chinese food is better,' the Tai Tai smiled, her hands on her hips. 'But then why should the maomi be any different?' She turned towards a shelf and took down a box with Maomi Deluxe printed in big characters on it. The camera zoomed in on the box.

It hurt me to breathe. Soyabean would have to eat whatever was in there. But what if Liu Laoban had forgotten to switch the food?

The Tai Tai tossed out the food that Old Lu had put out for Soyabean and poured in the contents of the Maomi Deluxe box instead. Soyabean jerked his head up excitedly and ran towards the bowl. His fur bounced up and down in a shiny halo. He buried his mouth deep in the bowl and began to gobble greedily.

The camera moved away from the scene on the stage and swept across the audience. They looked transfixed. A few were mouthing the punch line of the ad in anticipation, 'Chinese food for Chinese cat because after all Chinese food is better.'

I glimpsed a close-up of Liu Laoban. He was smiling so much I could almost smell his foul breath.

And then in an instant his smile crumbled. A shocked cry rippled across the room. The camera swung unsteadily back to the stage to reveal Soyabean thrashing around the stage, foaming at the mouth. He flapped about pathetically. The Ren actors on the stage stood helplessly by as though paralyzed.

Then Soyabean scrambled shakily onto his paws. He looked directly into the camera, eyes staring wildly, ears flattened, and opened his mouth. A stream of vomit came shooting out.

The audience erupted in a roar.

'Soyabean has been poisoned! Maomi Deluxe is poisoned cat food. Hundreds of cats have already died eating it. You've all just seen for yourself what happens when a cat eats it!' It was Madam Wang. She was on her feet, shouting.

She had understood. The plan was working! The ball was rolling!

I leapt off the sofa and began pacing up and down in front of the TV set. Behind me Auntie Li was jabbering away hysterically but I was too focussed on what was going on, on the screen to pay her attention.

People were rushing on to the stage now. I tried to look out for Mr and Mrs A but I couldn't see them amongst the mass of Ren crushed up against each other.

Many people had begun to yell out accusations. 'My cat died of kidney failure three weeks after she began eating Maomi Deluxe. Arrest Liu Libo. Throw him into jail. Punish those responsible,' an elderly lady bellowed.

'My little Sugarcane is sick too. I've been buying Maomi Deluxe for him for a month. He was always healthy before but now he vomits all the time. Just like Soyabean. Arrest Liu Libo. Punish those responsible,' another Ren called out.

A chant rose up. 'Punish those responsible. Punish those responsible.'

Just then a terrifying cacophony of meows joined in the general mayhem. Several Ren screamed and jumped up on chairs. It was the Ghost Street gang boys. Da Ge, Soyabean's Ba and a dozen other dustbin cats came charging down the aisles and made straight for Liu Laoban and Xiao Xu.

The two men were chalk-white. Liu Laoban was holding his arms out trying to push away the mob of Ren advancing on him. 'Now, now,' he was saying, barely audible above the noise. 'Calm down everybody. Keep calm. I'm sure there's a reasonable explanation for what happened just now.'

At the same time Xiao Xu was trying to worm his

way out of the crowd. He had a hunted, trapped look in his eyes. But before he could get very far a great big orange cat leapt onto his face with a blood-curdling yowl and scratched him with a mighty swipe.

It was Soyabean's Ba.

Xiao Xu fell to the floor, clutching his face, howling in pain. A crowd of angry Ren fell upon him. And that was the last I saw of him that evening.

There was only one further shot of the Advertising Council President, his flabby cheeks flapping in panic, frantically gesturing at the camera before the TV screen went blank.

chapter thirteen

SOYABEAN

Hutong Hero

I had spent the morning chasing the sun. It wasn't easy to stay with the lone, watery beam as it bounced around the courtyard. It needed skill and determination. But luckily, that wasn't a problem for me. I was a quickest one after all. And I liked to be warm.

This morning's breakfast sat comfortably heavy in my stomach. Auntie Li had been cooking me extra special meals now that I was a hero. Sometimes I got yoghurt for dessert three times a day. Even Mrs A seemed to have forgotten all about the awful starvation diet Chen Daifu had encouraged her to put me on.

It was just as well. I needed to eat to keep my energy levels up. Being such a big celebrity was terribly exhausting. More people than ever before wanted to meet me now. What with the photo shoots and interviews I scarcely had time to stalk birds or just lounge in bed anymore.

I wasn't even able to see much of Tofu. There were always so many strange Ren around she was usually off hiding in corners. But sometimes at night she would come find me to cuddle or if she wasn't sleepy to stalk me like when we were kittens.

It could be quite irritating the way she would jump right off a high table and land on my tummy, just as I was about to doze off and get some hard-earned rest. But I would forgive her because it was rare to find her in a playful mood.

For the first few days after the awards ceremony we'd had so many visitors landing up at the siheyuan that Mrs A had decided to let people in only if they made a prior appointment.

This morning had been relatively quiet with just the one meeting with Fat Tao. He had been pestering Auntie Li for days to be allowed to come over and Mrs A had finally given in.

What a different figure he'd cut today compared to the last time he'd come by, full of threats and carrying that dreadful poster of the cat on a plate. His eyes had been downcast and his shoulders stooped without a hint of aggression. I think he may even have had a bath. He certainly smelt a lot better than before.

He'd brought along a thousand-year-old egg for me as a present. Now, that didn't persuade me to actually like him, but I couldn't help melting just a tiny bit. Thousand-year-old eggs were delicious. They weren't really a 1000 years old, you see. That would be disgusting. They were just called that because the yummy green yolk and dark brown outsides made them look aged.

'So, Fat Tao,' Mrs A had said coldly when Auntie Li led him into the courtyard. 'Come again to warn us about the cats? Or is to tell us how dirty they are?'

'Nothing like that Tai Tai,' Fat Tao had mumbled, looking at his toes. 'Just brought a small token of my affection for your maomi. We're all so grateful for what he has done.'

He'd then held out the thousand-year-old egg towards me.

It was quite amazing. Only a moment before I had been thinking about how full I'd felt. Breakfast had been particularly large. But suddenly I'd found myself hungry again. That was the magic of thousand-year-old eggs.

Fat Tao was probably the last of the neighbours to have come around to see me. Not only was everyone excited that I'd helped uncover the Maomi Deluxe fraud but what they were really grateful about was the fact that the government was finally building a brand new five-star toilet for our hutong.

It was going to have foot-operated flushes and

running hot water. Xiao Wang was forever describing the wonders of the new toilet-to-be to Mrs A when he came by, which was nearly every day.

His Ma had decided to wait for a bit before getting him his own pet cat, she'd been so shaken up by the Maomi Deluxe affair. He was disappointed, but Mrs A had told him he could come around and play with Tofu and me whenever he liked.

But by far the greatest numbers of visitors were Ren from Madam Wang's cat protection society. For the first week or so after we had exposed Liu Laoban's scam, they came to the courtyard in excited droves. Some had tears in their eyes as they hugged Mrs A. 'Soyabean has saved us,' they would say.

I was flattered. My role in the whole affair had undoubtedly been crucial. But I was also a little worried. There was still no news about what was actually going to happen to Xiao Xu and Liu Laoban.

Even though it was clear to everyone after my performance that something was wrong with Maomi Deluxe, Liu Laoban was a rich Ren. He had a lot of guanxi, connections, in high-up places.

Mr and Mrs A were often huddled around the newspaper with Auntie Li, all of them looking worried and talking in hushed tones. 'Can they really let the rascals off after all the proof against them?' Mrs A had once asked, shaking her head in disgust.

'Money can turn black into white in this dirty world,' Auntie Li had muttered in reply.

The newspapers were full of stories of Ren protesting in the streets. It had all begun with members of Madam Wang's Capital Animal Welfare Association holding up banners and marching up and down outside Tiananmen Square.

I had never been to this Square but Da Ge told us that the Ghost Street gang boys knew it well. It was enormous. A cat would loose his breath running from one side to another before he'd even got half way across. And it was right in the centre of Beijing, near where Ren who belonged to the government worked.

There were pictures of the Square in the newspaper every day now. Madam Wang's group was always featured with red banners painted with slogans like 'Down with Liu Libo; Cat Murderer, Societal Leach,' or 'Punish Liu Libo; Enemy of the Old Hundred Names.'

Tofu was confused by the 'Old Hundred Names' bit. 'What does that mean?' she'd asked, her small face wrinkled with puzzlement.

Mrs A was right, I'd thought. Tofu really was a Baby Cat. Fancy, not knowing something as simple as that! Hadn't her Ma taught her anything? But then, I felt guilty because of course her Ma was a dustbin cat and probably not all that well educated.

'The Old Hundred Names,' I had explained to her patiently, 'refers to the ordinary people of China because almost all Ren in China share around 100 family names. Like Li and Wang.'

'What about Liu and Xu?' she'd said.

'Yes, yes, those too.'

'Soyabean, why don't cats have family names?'

Tofu's questions could be quite difficult. Luckily, I hadn't had to answer that one because Mr A had switched on the TV and everyone had run over to it, to watch the latest news from Tiananmen Square.

Bigger and bigger crowds had begun to join Madam Wang's friends. But these new Ren didn't seem particularly interested in Liu Laoban and Maomi Deluxe. Groups of Dustbin Ren made an appearance. 'Pay us our salaries now!'; 'Society owes a debt to migrant sweat!' their placards read.

We watched an interview on TV with a construction worker at the Stadium who said that his laoban had not paid him a single Yuan for the last five months. The Ren was so thin it hurt to just look at him.

He told the TV reporter that when he'd finally had the courage to ask for his salary, the laoban had fired him and told him to go back to his village. But the Ren didn't even have the money to buy a train ticket home. 'I don't mind eating bitterness, but this is worse than slavery,' he'd said, anger dancing in his eyes.

Tofu was forever looking out for a glimpse of Four Fingers Fu. But she never did spot him.

In the meantime the crowds at Tiananmen kept swelling. There were groups of elderly Ren complaining that something called their 'pensions' were not being paid by the government. Others were unhappy about having been forced to move out of their homes so that stadiums for the big Games could be built on that land.

This afternoon, long after Fat Tao had gone and I had taken a longish-afternoon nap following a wholly satisfying lunch of fried fish and yoghurt, we heard the usual cry from the street outside.

'Wan Bao, Wan Bao, Beijing Wan Bao!'

It was the newspaper Ren who went cycling around the hutongs every afternoon carrying stacks of Beijing Wan Bao, the Beijing Evening News. Auntie Li went out to get us our copy for the day, but when she returned she was looking unusually excited.

'Look!' she said running up to Mrs A who was sitting in front of the computer in the study. 'The Premier is going to make a speech on TV tomorrow. About that murderer Liu Libo and Maomi Deluxe.'

For the rest of the day, everyone kept dashing around, chattering and making phone calls. Madam Wang called several times and Auntie Li nipped out to gossip with the hutong neighbours. It took me a while to figure out what the big deal was but by listening carefully to the As' conversations I gathered that a Premier was a very powerful Ren in the government.

Mr A said that his speech would finally reveal what the government's decision on Liu Laoban's punishment was. I skipped about, my tail swishing. I couldn't wait to find out. Nor seemingly, could anyone else.

Auntie Li came back from her gossip session with the neighbours to inform us that Old Lady Fang from the corner store had decided to hook up her TV set out in the alleyway. The neighbours had decided to watch the Premier's speech together.

'Is it okay if I join them, tomorrow?' Aunti Li asked Mrs A.

'Is it alright if we join too?' Mrs A asked back.

In the end Mr and Mrs A, Auntie Li, Tofu and me, all went out into the hutong along with the neighbours the next morning. It was a cold, windy day but everyone pressed together to keep warm. Someone had put out a few low stools on the road and these were offered to the As. Mrs A sat down, but Mr A insisted on standing.

Hot, roasted chestnuts were passed around and to my delight a jian bing maker from down the road had come along as well and was handing out the yummiest, eggy, pancakes.

Many of the neighbours made it a point to give my chin a scratch and offer me a bite of jian bing. I was very popular you see; a hutong hero.

Xiao Wang took me into his lap and his Ma gave me an extra bite of jian bing. Fat Tao, who was sitting on a stool a little distance away from the rest of the neighbours nodded in my direction in a not too unfriendly way.

Tofu had wandered off inside the store where she was busy cuddling up to that yappy dog, Eraser. I still didn't know what she saw in him. Personally, I thought him quite an unattractive creature. But I suppose he wasn't too bad, for a dog.

He was suitably well mannered around me. Bobbing his head up and down and grinning humbly. Tofu had told me that he was in awe of me. I'd realized then, that he couldn't be totally stupid.

'Shhh!' someone suddenly shushed. 'It's about to start!' Old Lady Fang turned up the TV volume and all of us craned our necks forward to see as best as we could. The TV screen was much smaller than the As' and the picture was less clear. But nonetheless I could make out a serious looking Ren with big glasses sitting behind a desk.

In front of him was a low arrangement of pink flowers, behind him a Chinese flag. He began to speak, slowly, staring directly into the camera.

'My fellow countrymen and countrywomen,' he said. 'I have taken this extraordinary measure of speaking to all of you directly today because I realize that many of you have concerns that need to be addressed.'

'You may believe that your leaders, your Party, is not aware or perhaps does not care about the many, difficult problems you face. Let me assure you, that this is absolutely untrue.'

'Your comrades in the Party have been up day and

night ever since the dreadful corruption of one of our so called 'model' businessmen, Liu Libo, came to light.'

'We have been trying to understand how his illegal and harmful actions could have been allowed unchecked for so long. Not only that, we have also been devising ways to ensure that it is never allowed to happen again.'

A cheer rose up in the hutong, mingled with what distinctly sounded like meows. I looked around this way and that until I saw Da Ge and Ba. They were squatting on the roof of the house opposite Old Lady Fang's shop, listening intently.

Ba's ears seemed to be missing even more bits than usual but he looked more handsome than ever. My heart swelled with pride.

'Not only that,' the Premier went on. 'But also to make sure that the public enemy Liu Libo and his associates are appropriately punished in accordance with the full force of the law of the People's Republic of China.'

More cheers from the neighbours and the stamping of boots.

'The law that is here to protect each and every one of you, my fellow citizens and comrades. We, your leaders, are not unaware of the numerous difficulties you face in your day-to-day lives. China is still a developing country. Her problems are multifold. But thanks to you, the Chinese people; thanks to your ability to work hard and eat bitterness, we can promise you that the future of this country and of your children will be brighter than you can imagine.'

The hutong was ringing with supportive cries. Old Lady Fang was dabbing at her eyes. Even Fat Tao looked moved, his usual sour expression brightened by the enthusiasm flushed across his face.

'I ask for your support and for your patience. Your Party will not let you down. Many of you have suffered at the hands of that scoundrel Liu Libo. You have bought his sub-standard apartments; you have fed your pets his poisoned food.'

'But thanks to the efforts of the brave and noble cat Soyabean, we are going to make sure that an end is put to this. Society will have nothing more to fear from the likes of Liu. The Supreme People's Court of the People's Republic of China has found Liu Laoban guilty of grievous wrong to society and sentenced him to fifteen years in jail. His associate known as Xiao Xu has also been sentenced to a minimum of five years in prison.'

'I hope to have restored your trust in your leaders and Party. Xie! Xie! And have a good day.' As the Premier disappeared from the screen, the hutong was silent as though collectively holding its breath. I was holding my breath too. My ears were ringing, my blood thudding.

Had I heard correctly? Had the Premier, China's top leader, really called *me* a brave and noble cat?

Had he really said the word 'Soyabean'? The roar from the neighbours that began a few seconds later confirmed that he had.

Mrs A turned to me and held me up high. 'Oh!,' she gasped. 'My hero.' Her voice was almost drowned out by the flood of congratulations that everyone was shouting out in my direction.

'We were just run-of-the-mill laobaixing before,' said Xiao Wang's Ma, battling her way through the crowd to pat my head. 'But now we can be proud to say we are friends of a hero that none less than the Premier has praised! It's unbelievable.'

Treats were thrust at me from all directions: a chestnut, half a jian bing, one of Old Lady Fang's pots of fresh yoghurt. I glanced up towards the roof. Ba was looking directly at me. He gave me a slow wink. And while he was too far away for me to swear it, I thought his eyes looked wetter than usual.

It was the happiest moment of my whole life.

Later that day as I lay in the siheyuan kitchen, panting with the exhaustion of having eaten several lunches, Mr and Mrs A discussed Liu Laoban's punishment. 'Guanxi or not, it looks like Liu really is in trouble. Fifteen years is a long time,' said Mr A.

'It's thanks to Madam Wang,' mused Mrs A. 'Her spirit mobilized all the laobaixing fed up of the petty corruption they face everyday.' 'Yes, I suppose it became too risky politically with so many groups of unhappy protestors for Liu to be allowed to get away,' said Mr A.

'He's, only the scapegoat,' interjected Auntie Li from the far corner where she was stacking plates. 'There are ten thousand Lius in China. But the government's always operated like this. Kill the rooster to scare the monkey. That's the way of this country.'

'Well Auntie Li, these were certainly 'roosters' we could all well do without,' said Mrs A smiling. But then her face clouded over. 'I can't imagine how dreadful Nai Nai must feel. After all, however crooked that Xiao Xu might be, he is her grandson. I should call her. I've been meaning to for days. It's worrying that we haven't heard anything from her. She's probably the only person in the city who hasn't been around to see Soyabean.'

Mrs A's words cut through my haze of satisfaction like a cleaver. It was true. I hadn't heard any news of Nai Nai since the awards show. The last time I'd seen her I'd still been on the stage at the ceremony, dripping in vomit, watching the pandemonium below as the audience attacked Liu Laoban and Xiao Xu.

Right after Ba had scratched Xiao Xu in the face to prevent him sneaking away, Madam Wang had beaten him to the ground with her handbag. Nai Nai had gone very still when she saw her grandson being led away, his lip bloody, by a security guard. She'd looked broken. And then someone had come and carried me off stage, away from the chaos, and I hadn't seen Nai Nai since.

I didn't sleep well that night. Partly, it may have been the overeating but images of Nai Nai also kept floating around in my head and I spent more time tossing and turning than asleep.

Early the next morning Mrs A called out to me as I was stretching on the living room sofa, trying to shake off the previous night's tiredness. 'Soyabean. Lai ba, come!' she said, her voice still clotted with sleep.

I trotted off to find her lying in bed. It was a perfect invitation for a further lie-in. As I snuggled into her warm body, she tickled my ears, lazily. I began purring so hard the vibrations filled the whole room. 'Soyabean,' Mrs A murmured into my neck, 'We're going to see your Nai Nai this morning.'

I paused mid-purr and jerked my head up. She smiled. 'You'd like that wouldn't you? I spoke to her last night and she invited us to come by. We're going to see your Nai Nai.'

Her voice softened. 'And of course your Ma will be there too.'

Ma! Just the sound of that word was enough to make me want to somersault around the room; to stalk dragonflies and slay rats; to bury my face in Ma's sweet, soft fur, the one place in the World where nothing bad could ever happen.

Two hours or so later I was in the car with Mrs A, twitching with impatience. My face glued to the window, I saw the shuttered restaurants on Ghost

Street zoom past, the red lanterns that decorated their fronts swinging in the wind. There was no sign of Ba or any of the Ghost Street gang.

It was only a few minutes drive from our hutong to East Drum Tower Avenue and a few more seconds to the Xu family's siheyuan in the hutong where I had been born.

The worn wooden doors to the courtyard opened even before Mrs A had finished parking the car. Nai Nai looked older, more wrinkled and worn out than I remembered. But then she held out her arms towards me and smiled.

'Maomi, what a big boy you've become,' she said. I was in her arms before she could finish, feeling the familiar dry, soft touch of her hands, inhaling her clean Nai Nai scent.

'Qing jin, come in,' Nai Nai said, beckoning Mrs A. And we all went in with Nai Nai cushioning me in her arms like she used to when I was a very small kitten.

'My son and his family are not at home,' Nai Nai said as she led Mrs A to the front room. 'They couldn't bear the looks of the neighbours any more. And the government is likely to launch an investigation into Lao Xu's own business dealings. They've gone south, to our relatives in Hangzhou.'

Nai Nai's tone was matter of fact, flat.

'I'm so sorry Madam Xu,' said Mrs A. 'You didn't deserve any of this.'

Nai Nai sighed heavily as she offered Mrs A a cup of hot tea. 'There is a saying in China, Mrs A. "White wine turns a man's face red, yellow gold turns his heart black." I always knew no good would come of that boy. Still, one couldn't help hoping that one was wrong.'

I was curled around Nai Nai's feet and couldn't see her face, but her hands were dangling slackly by her sides. Mrs A got down on her knees and gathered Nai Nai's hands into her own. She didn't say anything, but her silence was warm and comforting.

Finally I couldn't bear the quiet any more and meowed out loudly. Nai Nai picked me up again. 'So maomi, still a chatterbox, I see. Impatient, as always; my little Emperor!'

She tapped my nose.

'I'm proud of you little one. You have a brave heart.' The biggest lump began growing in my throat. I was a big cat now. And like Nai Nai had said, a brave cat. I fought to keep the lump down, but it kept rising. Then, just as the tears started to force their way out Nai Nai put me down on the floor.

'There's someone who is waiting to meet you,' she said and nodded her head towards the courtyard outside. Ma! Where was she?

I went bounding out of the room, into the yard and there were a dozen or so of my cousins sitting expectantly, bunched up together. 'Here he is!' one of them cried. 'Soyabean! The hero!'

And immediately the whole group charged at me. Before I knew it I was in a jumble of paws, whiskers, tails, laughing till I had no breath left.

'Son,' a meow cut through the ruckus. 'My son.'

I shrugged my cousins off and scrambled to my feet. There she was, golden and beautiful, exactly the way I remembered her. 'Ma!' I meowed, and the sound that came out sounded not like the roar of a hero but the mewl of a baby. 'Come here child,' she said, her voice as soothing as a spring breeze. 'How fine you look. And how fine you are.'

We spent the rest of the morning together Ma and me, sitting back on our haunches in the corner of the yard that used to my home. She said she got regular news of me from Ba.

'I worried so much when I heard you were caught up in some scheme with Xiao Xu. How could you have trusted him? I had warned you away from him since the day you opened your eyes,' she said, her eyes glowing with reproach.

I didn't know where to look. I knew I had been a foolish cat. I had made many mistakes. But everything was on the right track again. 'Don't worry, Ma. I'm a hero now,' I told her. 'The Premier himself said so.'

Ma seemed unimpressed. 'Hmph' she grumbled. 'And aren't you a bit chubby for a hero?' She could be so difficult, my Ma! But she *was* proud of me. I could tell by the way her ears smiled, lifting up gently around the edges whenever she looked at me.

She nibbled at my cheek. I swatted at hers. The bamboo thicket in the courtyard had dried up in the cold. But I could swear I heard the buzzing of a dragonfly somewhere.

When Mrs A and Nai Nai came out to the yard a while later to say it was time to leave, Ma turned her golden gaze at me. 'Man zou, little one, go slowly,' she said, echoing her farewell to me those many months ago, when I had first left here for Mr and Mrs A's siheyuan.

'And always remember, the taste of a dumpling can't be judged by how well it's folded.'

I thought about her parting words on the way back to our hutong. They sounded very wise. The only problem was that I usually ate up a dumpling so quickly, I didn't have the time to notice how it was folded.

chapter fourteen

TOFU

Yunqi

A great squall of excitement had burst over us since the day of the awards ceremony. Soyabean was a national celebrity. Liu Laoban and Xiao Xu were in jail. Our once-peaceful courtyard home was overrun with visitors.

But I was in the quiet space at the centre of the storm. I worried about Mama. Madam Wang had told us she lived with Old Man Zhao now. But she also said that Mama had been ill. Old Man Zhao had been feeding her Maomi Deluxe for a few weeks, before Madam Wang warned him to stop but it had been too late.

Mama's kidneys were damaged. She was better now and Mrs A had promised Madam Wang we would go visit her soon. But for the moment every one was too busy celebrating to care about much else.

There were many matters to celebrate, of course. The bing du virus had faded away. Fat Tao went about carrying 1000-year-old eggs as treats these days instead of brandishing threatening posters. There were no more cat and dog kidnappings.

The As' friend, Mr J was back in Beijing. He'd come over for dinner the other day, grinning sheepishly. 'Yes, maybe I overreacted,' he'd admitted to Mr A. 'The worst case scenarios didn't play out, but you've got to admit it was touch and go for a while.'

'You have no idea how true that is,' Mrs A had interrupted moodily. I'd known she was thinking about what had happened to me.

'Anyway, you've all got something to thank me about,' Mr J had grinned, changing the topic. He'd scooped up Soyabean who was curled up at his feet and held him up high.

'Don't you remember, it was I who had first suggested your gorgeous Soyabean would do well as a cat model?'

'Yes,' replied Mrs A, sharply. 'And look at the crooks your little suggestion ended up getting us involved with.' 'Aha!' Mr J said. 'But look at how cleverly those crooks have been brought down. Thanks to our golden hero.' Soyabean who'd been stretched out across Mr J's arms had meowed loudly in agreement.

'I could swear sometimes that these cats

understand every word we say,' Mr A had said staring at Soyabean curiously. I'd been crouching under the living room coffee table, but Soyabean's eyes sought me out. Our tails had traced a smile in the air.

But even though there was a lot to smile about, so much was still so wrong. There were all the pet owners whose animals had died because of Maomi Deluxe. Their cats wouldn't come back to life just because Liu Laoban had been punished.

And Four Fingers Fu and the other dustbin Ren were probably still drinking away long, sad nights in their smelly shack. I had looked very hard for them when the protests at Tiananmen Square were shown on TV, but I hadn't been able to glimpse anyone I knew.

I did meet with Eraser sometimes, though not very often. The last time was when we were all gathered outside Old Lady Fang's xiao mai bu to watch the Premier's speech. When the Premier singled out Soyabean to thank, the hutong had gone wild. I had stepped back into the shop to get away from all the noise. The faces of the Ren had turned purple as they shouted out their congratulations to Soyabean.

It had made me quite uncomfortable. I'd seen how changeable Ren were. They were not like cats. They could say one thing, but mean something else. Their lips could smile even when their eyes told another story.

Eraser had joined me at the back of the shop

where we'd stood amidst packets of biscuits and noodles. 'Are you okay Tofu,' he'd yapped, snout quivering with concern.

'Yes, of course,' I'd replied, suddenly feeling tired. I hadn't realized how keyed up I'd been over the last few weeks. The uncertainty over Liu Laoban and Xiao Xu's fate had been draining.

'You're not jealous, are you?' Eraser had then asked. My tail had shot up in surprise. Jealous? Why in the World? 'Whatever do you mean?' I'd said.

Eraser had looked all solemn and touched his nose to mine. 'I don't think it's fair how Soyabean gets all the credit for everything. After all, it was you who came up with the plan, not him. You're the real hutong hero, even though no one realizes it.' The dog had actually begun to choke up.

'Oh Eraser!' I'd almost laughed out aloud but controlled myself because I'd realized he was taking this very seriously. 'You have no idea how very relieved I am that it's not me out there being jumped on by all those Ren. And Soyabean deserves all the congratulations he gets because only he could have pulled off my plan.'

'But it was *your* plan.' Eraser's lower lip had jutted out; his most stubborn look.

'Yes, it was. But what's a plan, little friend? It's nothing but a thought inside your head. Without Soyabean's confidence and talent, Liu Laoban and Xiao Xu would still be out there murdering cats with their poisoned food, regardless of however many plans I might have had. I could never have vomited with such conviction as did Soyabean. It took real skill.'

The dog had snorted as though unconvinced but hadn't pursued the conversation further. I'd felt a quick stab of affection for him. He was a loyal friend.

This morning I had sniffed Spring in the air; the smell of dust and earth. I remembered how my brothers and I used to huddle inside the dustbin in Old Man Zhao's backyard when the dust storms raged so hard that the whole World turned orange.

It had been a year ago. I hadn't realized how much could happen in a year. I was a grown up cat now. Although Da Ge still liked to call me 'kid'. He visited every once in a while with news of the outside World. He talked about crab-catching expeditions the Ghost Street gang organized every time one of the restaurants on the street received a fresh batch of hairy crabs to cook up in spicy sauce.

He told me about the continuing attempts of the Big Stone Bridge boys to take over the Ghost Street gang's territory. 'You should have seen how I scratched the rascal's whiskers out, Number Three,' he would boast, showing off his latest battle scars. 'You would have been proud of me, kid.'

And I was. I knew I had the bravest, big brother in the World.

I was hoping he might come by this evening. It had been a few days since we'd chatted last.

I climbed up the pomegranate tree. Little green sprouts had begun to spring up along its branches making them less poky. In a few months the tree would hang heavy with fruit again. It was something nice to look forward to.

I spotted Soyabean fast asleep on the kitchen window sill. He looked plump and peaceful. Auntie Li was frying up some chicken liver in the kitchen for our supper that evening. A sparrow was flitting about the roof, but I felt too lazy to pay it much attention.

Outside the courtyard a Ren was cycling around in the hutong, tinkling his bell and shouting out, 'Window cleaner! I can clean your dirty windows!'

I could hear the clink of Mahjong pieces being shaken up. A new game must have been about to begin outside Old Lady Fang's xiao mai bu. I put my head down between my front paws. My eyes felt soft with sleep.

I was a lucky cat. Madam Wang had been the first to say it. 'Maomi, your yunqi is very good,' she'd said as Mr and Mrs A had carried me away from the dustbin. But what a strange thing yunqi was. It could come and it could go just as easily. You could never quite wrap your paws around it I thought. A moment later, I was fast asleep.

GLOSSARY

Beijing Wan Bao	:	Beijing Evening News (a newspaper)
Bing du	:	Virus
Cai gou	:	Literally 'food dog'; used to denote the kind of dog that is traditionally eaten in China (as opposed to dogs that are kept as pets)
Daifu	:	Doctor
Da Ge	:	Older brother
Dajia	:	Everyone
Da Luan	:	Chaos
Gan bei	:	Literally 'dry glass'; used as an equivalent for bottoms up
Ge men(r)	:	Mate, informal for close friend
Guanxi	:	Connections
Huai Dan	:	Literally 'bad egg,' a derogatory term
Huan ying	:	Welcome
Huang Shu Lang	:	Chinese weasel
Hutong	:	Alleyway (specific to the old city of Beijing)
Jian bing	:	Egg pancake, common Beijing street food

Kai	:	Open
Ku	:	Cool (in the slangy sense of approval)
Lai	:	Come (imperative)
Lao	:	Old
Laobaixing	:	Literally 'old hundred names'; used as an equivalent of the 'common man'
Laoban	:	Boss
Liulangmao	:	Stray cat
Luan	:	chaos
Man Zou	:	Literally 'go slowly,' used as a common farewell
Maomi	:	Kitten
Mei shi(r)	:	No problem
Men(r)	:	Door
Nai Nai	:	Paternal grandmother
Ni hao	:	Used as a greeting, the equivalent of 'hello'
Nongmin gong	:	Migrant workers
Pengyou	:	Friend
Qing jin	:	An invitation to 'come in' or 'enter'
Qipao	:	A tight-fitting, one-piece dress for women
Ren	:	Person
Siheyuan	:	Courtyard house
Tai keqi le	:	Phrase meaning, a great pity
Tai Tai	:	Mistress
Tu	:	Dirt, soil
Waidi	:	Non-local
Wai guo	:	Foreign

Xiao	:	Small or young
Xiao mai bu	:	Small corner store
Xiao xin	:	Literally 'small heart'; the equivalent of warning somebody to 'be careful'
Xie Xie	:	Thank You
Yunqi	:	Luck

A 'r' sound is usually added to word endings in the Beijing dialect. So that for example 'men' or door is pronounced as 'menr' in Beijing. This is what Tofu commented on as Da Ge's strange new accent in chapter four.

I have used the pinyin system of romanising Chinese which is currently the standard form in mainland China.

ACKNOWLEDGEMENTS

Thanks are due to the following people: Kiran Ganguli, Maya Naidoo, Tuva Kahrs, Deboleena Mazumdar, Janie Yu, Stephanie Ollivier, Cathy Kohler, Wang Wanying, Martine Torfs and Jehangir Pocha. Li Ayi for her chicken livers and much else. My agent Jayapriya Vasudevan and editor at HarperCollins, V.K. Karthika for ensuring a butter-like smoothness to the passage of this book. Gerolf Van de Perre, illustrator extraordinaire, for instinctively grasping with feline perspicacity the world according to Soyabean and Tofu. My brother Shekhar and father Swaminathan for encouraging with kind words and sage advice. My cats, the very golden Caramel and very wise Tofu, for providing flesh and blood prototypes, snuggles and whiskered kisses. Julio, my husband and inspiration, for looking after said cats when I was busy writing and guiding the whole literary process with the flair of a circus master. Ishaan, my toddling son, and latest addition to the family zoo, for learning with time to be gentle with the cats and granting his mama an hour or two of keyboard time every once in a while. My mother, Gitanjali, for planting the seed that grew into this book. To her, as always, my deepest thanks.

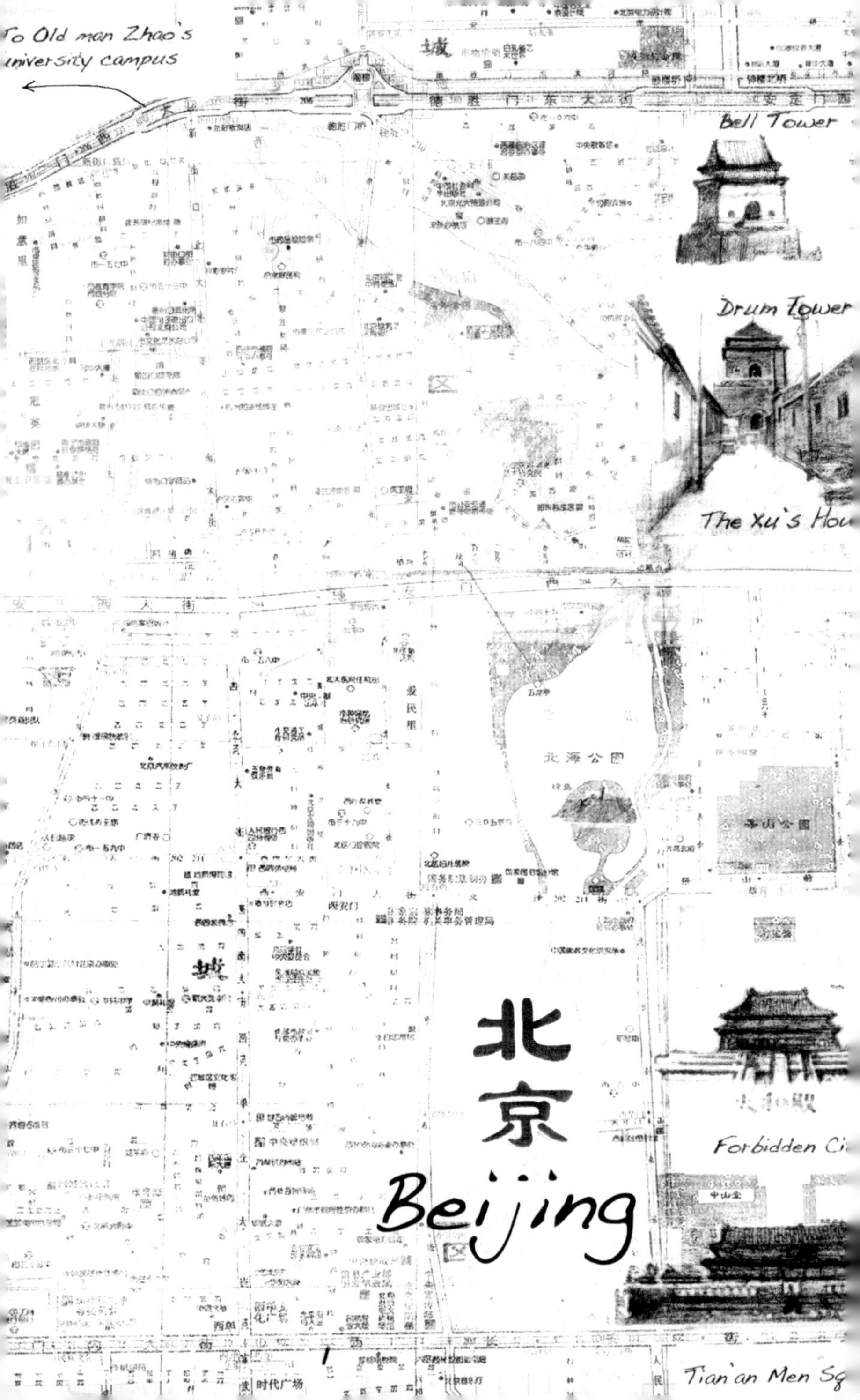

To Old man Zhao's university campus
Bell Tower
Drum Tower
The Xu's Hou
北海公园
西安门
北京
Beijing
Forbidden Ci
中山堂
时代广场
Tian'an Men Sq